Alone—Together

"*Are you sure we can't get back to Killara to-night?*" Diana asked hesitantly, with an uneasy look around the deserted cabin.

"Not unless you happen to have a couple of spotlights with you," Matt said casually. "There isn't any moonlight, and I don't fancy riding down that trail when it's as black as the inside of a hat. We can leave in the morning as soon as it's light."

He poured some brandy into his coffee. "Have some? It might warm you a bit. When that firewood goes, I'm afraid it's going to get mighty chilly in here."

"*What's the social etiquette for an unplanned overnight stay in the woods?*" Diana tried to keep her voice even. "*Do we huddle on the hearth watching the warm coals die?*"

"I think it would be more practical to roll out that sleeping bag of mine. Fortunately, it's double-size so sharing it shouldn't be too bad!"

LOVE'S HIDDEN FIRE

by
Glenna Finley

A SIGNET BOOK

SIGNET
Published by the Penguin Group
Penguin Books USA Inc., 375 Hudson Street,
New York, New York 10014, U.S.A.
Penguin Books Ltd, 27 Wrights Lane,
London W8 5TZ, England
Penguin Books Australia Ltd, Ringwood,
Victoria, Australia
Penguin Books Canada Ltd, 2801 John Street,
Markham, Ontario, Canada L3R 1B4
Penguin Books (N.Z.) Ltd, 182–190 Wairau Road,
Auckland 10, New Zealand

Penguin Books Ltd, Registered Offices:
Harmondsworth, Middlesex, England

First published by Signet, and imprint of New American Library, a division
of Penguin Books USA Inc.

First Printing, January, 1971
24   23   22   21   20   19   18

 REGISTERED TRADEMARK—MARCA REGISTRADA

Printed in the United States of America

For Donald

"Lay your hands there light, and yearn
   Till the yearning slips
   Through the finger tips
In a fire which a few discern
   And a very few feel burn
And the rest, they may live and learn!"
                    —Robert Browning

Chapter One

"What did you say he was?" Diana Burke asked incredulously, turning to look at her employer.

Until then, she had been leaning against the window casement staring down onto the tangled traffic of New York's upper Fifth Avenue and trying to ignore the instructions coming from the gray-haired man sitting at the desk behind her. Suddenly, despite her preoccupation, one of his phrases had penetrated her wall of reserve.

"You've got to be kidding!" she added definitely.

David Royle looked up from the letter he was reading. "What are you talking about now?" he asked in an indulgent tone.

"You were going on about this paragon I'm supposed to work for," she persisted impatiently as she walked back by his desk and perched on the arm of a chair facing him. "What did you say his job was?"

He stared at her. "I said that Matthew Reynolds was a parasitologist."

"That's what I thought you said the first time," she told him dispiritedly. "I'll bet you can't spell it."

His lips tightened. "Might I ask what this inane conversation is about?"

"Nothing, really." She sagged against the chair back. "Only I can't figure out why you pick on me, of all people, to fly across the continent up into a forsaken wilderness to be an interior decorator for some moldy old para . . . para . . ."

"Parasitologist."

". . . Parasitologist," she concluded defiantly. "Either I must have done a horrible job on Mrs. Robertson's penthouse last month or you can't stand having me around the firm any more."

Royle's forehead creased in amusement. "You know very well that you received a salary bonus for that penthouse job. That's why only your services will do for Mrs. Robertson's nephew and his ranch. What does Dr. Reynolds' occupation have to do with it?"

"I don't know." Diana slipped into a more comfortable position and pulled at her wool skirt so that her legs were a little more discreetly covered. "Maybe it's just that I don't want any part of him or the job. For one thing, I don't have a desire to go traveling right now. Heavens, I was six months in Lebanon last year working on the Beirut casino and then there was that hotel renovation in Trieste. Ever since I've been home, I've been working day and night on that darned penthouse decor . . ."

"I realize that," he murmured.

"So why can't you put somebody else on the nephew's ranchhouse, for pete's sake? Besides," she tilted her head impudently, "he probably wants the whole thing done in petrified wood paneling and is crazy about tables covered with oilcloth. I wouldn't last a weekend in those surroundings . . . you know I wouldn't."

He looked at her reprovingly. "My dear Diana, don't take me for a fool. I know perfectly well you can fit into whatever surroundings you find; that's one reason you've become so valuable to Royle Interiors. It's also the reason why you've come along so far in the five years you've been with us. But I also know that you're just twenty-five years old and if you continue at the rate you've been working, you'll be worn to a shadow by your next birthday. Therefore, you have to take some time to rest." He held up his hand as she started to interrupt. "I know what you're going to say; we haven't had any qualms about seeing that you had any time off so far but my guilty conscience is catching up with me." He ducked his chin down and peered at her over the tops of his glasses. "Even though I am an old fogey, I've enjoyed seeing that trim figure of yours flit around here. It's up to me to make sure that you keep right on."

"Now you're being silly."

"Am I?" he asked reprovingly. "I don't think

11

so. At least, I don't see any gray in those brown locks of yours yet."

"Heaven forbid!" She ran an impatient hand through her wavy hair and succeeded in attractively disarranging it in the process. "My working schedule seems to be turning your hair whiter, though." She moved restlessly. "There's no reason for a health lecture now. You're making me sound like some neurotic idiot."

"I certainly don't mean to. I'm very fond of you and you know it. If I were thirty years younger, I'd be declaring my honorable intentions. But since I'm not thirty years younger and since you don't have any parents or available relatives nearby to ride herd on you, I'm taking over the job."

For the first time during the interview, Diana's lips curved into a soft smile. "And all this time, I thought you just liked me for the business I could bring into the firm," she chided gently.

"Don't think that didn't help," he admonished. "You don't stay on top in the decorating business without it. Besides, I'm not being completely altruistic, even now. Mrs. Robertson is in a position to throw a lot of future business our way if she stays happy with us."

"Do you mean that guest ranch of hers in Palm Desert?"

"Exactly, and I heard the other day that she's about to go to the Costa Smeralda in Sardinia to see about investing in real estate there." He leaned back in his desk chair. "So you, my dear, are off to redecorate a northwest ranch house."

"With the parasitologist."

"Without the parasitologist," he said reprovingly. "Dr. Reynolds is currently in the Aleutians on a research project and isn't expected back until the end of the summer. Mrs. Robertson wants the work done in his absence as a birthday present."

Diana pursed her lips in a silent whistle. "Some birthday present!"

David Royle allowed himself a wintry smile. "Exactly. The sky's the limit." He held up a brass key. "Here's a key to the ranch house. Our client will write to the foreman to tell him of your coming so that he can make the necessary arrangements."

"Where does this foreman live?"

"He has a separate cottage on the property. The rest of the help stay in a bunkhouse. Apparently the only ones who live in the main house are a cook and her niece, who will take care of your meals and handle the cleaning."

"It certainly sounds good . . ."

"That's what I told you."

". . . And dull," she said decisively. "You didn't let me finish my sentence. Where is this place, anyway?"

"Up by the Canadian border in Washington State." He checked the letter on his desk. "Deep in the Cascade Mountains."

"And how do I get there?" she said. "Pony express?"

"I believe the daily Boeing 707's are more reliable. They have electricity in that part of the country," he added with some sarcasm, "and the Indian reservations are few and far between."

Diana stood up and squared her shoulders. "What a pity. I was thinking of kerosene lamps in the shape of wigwams and tomahawks over the fireplace." She leaned over and took the key from him. "How long do I stay?"

"Until you put on ten pounds, at least, get some color in your cheeks . . ."

"And until I can transform the house into something bearable."

"Exactly . . . bringing back a nice profit for Royle Interiors."

She gave him a mocking salute. "So be it. I'm off as soon as I can get a plane reservation and stuff some blue jeans in my bag." Her smile flashed. "If I come back drawling and chewing hay straws, it will be all your fault."

He waved her out with a lazy gesture. "Just make sure you come back, my dear. Don't fall for any cowboys while you're out there."

"Cowboys! Heavens, you needn't worry." She paused in his doorway. "I don't even like Western movies on television." She blew him an airy kiss. "Keep a candle in the window to guide me back to civilization."

He watched her disappear down the corridor

and then put his client's letter carefully in his middle desk drawer. Perhaps I should have told her more about the place, he thought, staring down at the letter, instead of having her walk in with the wrong ideas. Then he shook his head and slowly closed the drawer. On the other hand, it wouldn't hurt the young lady to be taken down a peg or two and lose some of that brittle career-girl efficiency. No, it wouldn't hurt at all.

Two days later, Diana discovered that transportation to her wilderness involved a comfortable, if uneventful, jet take-off from Newark. In the big 707, she was seated next to an older woman who was returning to her home in Alaska after a visit to her married daughter in New York.

"I'm glad they serve breakfast on this flight," she told Diana after they had been aloft for a few minutes. "With a nine A.M. departure time, I thought we'd only have lunch."

"There's barely time for two meals," said a smiling stewardess as she leaned over to hand an attractive breakfast tray to Diana. "We land in Seattle just after one o'clock."

"That should be fine," the Alaskan said complacently and then as the hostess moved on down the aisle she leaned over and spoke confidentially to Diana. "I'm certainly all in favor of progress. It used to take so much longer to fly out West in the days of propeller planes. I think the most discouraging thing was that with the time changes, you kept getting the same meal all the time. I flew out of Bermuda once at the crack of dawn and changed planes in New York for the West. Before I got to Seattle, I had scrambled eggs for three consecutive meals." She looked down at the corn fritters and bacon in front of her with satisfaction. "I wouldn't have minded except that I can't stand scrambled eggs."

Diana smiled appreciatively. "I've heard of things like that. These days, you're fortunate to be able to eat and see the feature movie before you arrive." She sipped her coffee. "Be sure and tell me if there's anything special in the way of scenery." She glanced out the window carelessly. "Besides clouds, of course."

"I'll do that," the woman promised.

It was some hours later that Diana felt a gentle touch on her shoulder and stirred restlessly on the small pillow tucked under her head. She opened her eyes and blinked, trying to orient herself.

"The scenery's here," came a voice at her side. "I'd hate to have you miss Mount Rainier. We're lucky it's so clear today."

Diana sat up abruptly and put up a hand to smooth her hair. "I'd forgotten where I was. Goodness, if we're in the neighborhood of Mount Rainier, I must have slept longer than I thought."

"Well, you said you didn't want to bother

with lunch," her seatmate reminded her, "so I told the stewardess not to wake you."

"Thank you, I'm sure I needed the sleep more than the food," Diana said. She leaned over to peer out the window at the awe-inspiring snow-capped mountain rising from a cluster of rugged attendant peaks below. "So that's Mount Rainier . . . it's easy to understand why the Indians worshiped natural elements like mountains, isn't it?" She shifted in her seat to get a better look at the panorama. "What are all the rest of the peaks?"

"The Cascade range. Really, they're all a part of the Rockies. Rainier is over 14,000 feet high and probably one of the prettiest mountains in America because of its setting. Of course, the highest mountain is in my home state . . . that's Mt. McKinley at 20,320 feet. You'll have to come up and take a look at it."

"You Alaskans!" Diana shook her head in mock disbelief. "You talk about going thousands of miles as casually as a New Yorker talks of going to the Bronx. But I must admit that with scenery like that," she nodded toward the majestic, sunlit mountain now disappearing behind them, "it's worth it. The snow glistening through the cloud haze looks so untouched that it really seems out of this world, doesn't it?"

The older woman smiled. "Oh dear, it looks as if you're going to be another of them."

"Another what?"

"Scenery worshiper. I'd like to have a dollar for each of the folks who first come to this part of the country and then gradually fall under its spell; we have more transplanted Easterners than you'd believe. Most of the natives are saying it's getting too crowded and moving up Alaska way."

"Crowded!" Diana laughed and pointed down to the mountain range which was coming into sharper relief as the plane gradually descended. "You could drop all of greater New York into that and still hardly see your neighbor."

"Heaven forbid!" her seatmate said. "As far as neighbors go, it's enough to have them . . . we don't want to be able to see them. There goes the seat-belt sign; I think we're going to be bang on time."

"That's a blessing. I still have quite a way left to drive."

The older woman fumbled with her seat belt to pull it around her ample girth. "Which way do you head now?"

"Up by the Canadian border. Some isolated little ranch in the mountains."

The woman peered at her shrewdly. "Then you'll get some solitude, after all. There are some pretty big holdings up there."

"I doubt if this is one of them. At any rate, I don't intend to be there long enough for it to make much difference." Diana glanced through the window again. "It's starting to look like every other city now." Her sigh was almost unconscious. "What a pity! It was so beautiful back there by Mount Rainier."

"Wait until you see the scenery up by Mount Baker where you're going. Course it doesn't come up to Rainier's height but it's spectacular all the same. You might like that ranch more than you think."

"You seem bound to convert me." Diana flashed a conspirator's grin. "I'll tell you ... if I get too bored looking at the ranch hands, I'll go out and look at the scenery and store up for when I get back to Manhattan. My apartment there looks out onto the back of another apartment building."

"No mountains," the Alaskan lady said pointedly.

"No mountains." This time the grin was wry. "It's funny, I never thought about the view before."

"You will now, my dear," the other's tone was soft, "that's part of the spell."

The landing at Sea-Tac was strictly out of the pilot's manual, and on emerging from the big jet, Diana found the international terminal much like its many counterparts all over the world, groups of purposeful people whose preoccupied expressions showed that they were already halfway to their destination, a handful of soldiers sleeping in chairs and lounges under the watchful eye of a Traveler's Aid volunteer who was serving as their human alarm clock, the branch bank whose teller was efficiently coping with Far Eastern currency problems for Oriental departures and supplying American dollar bills for a tour group from Japan. Stand-up snack bars were thronged with customers snatching a quick cup of coffee, and a waiting line of patrons coiled in front of the dining room whose floor-to-ceiling windows over-looked the busy runways.

Diana finally located the car rental agency through which David Royle had made her res-ervations and some time later was being in-structed in the intricacies of the northern free-way which was to take her part of the way to her destination.

As she coped with trying to get on the busy eight-lane freeway she was thinking, "Back of beyond indeed! If I ever survive this traffic and succeed in getting off at the proper exit, I'll probably find that they're putting up a housing development next to the Reynolds' acreage. In-stead of packing blue jeans, I should have thrown in something snappy to wear to the neighborhood drive-in!"

Seattle was merely a glimpse of skyscrapers fronting onto a gigantic harbor as she drove through at sixty miles an hour. Ten minutes more and the freeway speed was raised to sev-enty. The dense population and suburban shopping centers thinned to frontage-road hamlets and then eventually to farm land and occasional dwellings as she continued to drive north.

After some hours of steady driving, she turned east off the freeway as her sketchy instructions ordered. A detour led to a wrong road and necessitated lengthy backtracking later in the day. The two-lane road deteriorated to a gravel surface as she made the final turn north again in the late afternoon. A small combination filling station and lunch counter was the only sign the neighborhood was inhabited, so she pulled in beyond the gas pump and got out of the car wearily.

The weatherbeaten door to the lunchroom opened and a grizzled face peered around the frame.

"Sorry but we're closed, ma'am," the man said. "My wife's off visitin' her relatives and I can't do any real cooking. I can let you have some gas, though, if that's what you're needin'."

Diana stayed by her open car door. "No thanks, I think I still have plenty of gasoline. I was hoping you could give me some directions along with a cup of coffee but I'll be happy to settle for just the directions." She consulted the letter that she had kept beside her on the front seat. "This is the Fruitland junction, isn't it?"

The man shifted a wad of something in his cheek and nodded slowly. "Yes ma'am."

"Well, I'm trying to get to a vacation cabin owned by Matthew Reynolds. It's called Killara and should be fairly close by."

"Vacation cabin?" His voice rose questioningly and he opened the door wider to poke his head further around the frame. "I know of Dr. Reynolds' place . . ."

"It must be the one I want." She checked the letter again. "The directions are a little vague after Fruitland junction. There's something about an unmarked turn onto a dirt road . . ."

He spit with unerring accuracy onto a drooping shrub at the corner of the building. "That's right. You go down this road about half a mile and turn onto the first dirt road to the right. Keep on it for about five miles and you'll come to Killara."

"How will I know it?"

"There ain't any other. Road stops when you get there." He looked at her carefully. "You expected?"

Her lips curved in amusement. "I should be. Why?"

"Just that they don't like strangers. Jim's had his orders."

"Jim?"

"Jim Dodge, the foreman." His forehead wrinkled in suspicion. "I thought you said you knew the folks."

"I said that I was expected," she told him, tossing the letter back onto the car seat. "First dirt road on the right, then. Thanks very much."

He started to withdraw his head like a turtle going back into his shell even before she could get back into the car. "Glad to oblige."

The filling station was the last sign of human habitation before the sharp turn onto a dirt track with a sifting of gravel along the tire ruts. As she eased the rental car into it and watched dust fill the twilight haze in her rear-vision mirror, she gave a sigh of regret that she hadn't changed clothes before the last leg of the trip. There was really no sense in getting her new orange knit filthy, to say nothing of her alligator pumps and bag. Her bone-colored sheared beaver jacket was on the back seat, but even so, the dust from the rough track would probably infiltrate the car. Blast Matthew Reynolds and his ranch house! She should have told David Royle that she would stay in the nearest motel and commute.

After the first half-mile, there was a heavier covering of gravel on the tracks and the dust abated. Then, after another period of climbing and twisting among the trees, the gravel overlay changed abruptly to hard surface.

"Curiouser and curiouser," Diana mused to herself. "Dr. Reynolds believes in doing himself well; a paved road to a vacation home. Nothing like roughing it in comfort. What on earth does a doctor of parasitology do on vacations? Try to find a sick parasite, of course!" And smiling at her feeble joke, she increased her speed as the road both leveled and straightened.

As the minutes went by, dusk seemed to hover at the top of the thick trees lining the road. She rolled down her window and sniffed appreciatively at the cool, sweet air filling the car. The muted noise of the car engine seemed to hang upon the stillness and Diana shivered involuntarily. This was getting away from the world with a vengeance!

And then suddenly the road emerged onto a grassy plateau rimmed with the forested prongs of mountain peaks. In the center of the plateau on a lush green lawn was a magnificent country manor house as carefully located at the base of the rugged wilderness range as a priceless gem would be placed in a unique setting.

A split-rail fence by the road bordered the lawn and fifty feet farther along two fieldstone posts marked the beginning of the winding drive up to the house.

She drove slowly through the entrance and up the drive. So this was Killara . . . the vacation house in the back of beyond! Either David Royle was indulging in a misplaced sense of humor or Dr. Matthew Reynolds was leading a far different holiday life than his aunt imagined.

The main wing of the manor house was a two-story structure of fieldstone and white-timbered siding. Two side wings were set slightly back from the main part which allowed a long loggia on either side. Comfortable-looking lounge furniture was scattered along these, providing bright spots of color against the gray stone background. Cedar shakes, mellowed and silvered with age, covered the gently sloping roofs and at the end of the main wing an enormous fieldstone chimney protruded. Long windows were flanked with wooden shutters of the same color tone as the roof. Banked rhododendrons at either end of the flagstone terrace in the front seemed as indigenous to the countryside as pots of red geraniums on the window sill of a stone house in Normandy.

By the time Diana had pulled her car up to the front door, ample time had passed for her to appreciate the fine architectural qualities of the house and wonder what in the world she was doing there. There was no reason to suppose that the interior of the dwelling was in any less perfect condition than the exterior and redecorating needlessly did not appeal to her. With an estate the size of the one in front of her, any projects undertaken would have to be lengthy, and if Dr. Reynolds were as great a dilettante as his aunt, she wouldn't be successful in the commission anyhow. When he finally returned home after his Alaskan sojourn, their coexistence on the premises would be too difficult to contemplate. But those thoughts were for the future and she needed something more tangible for the present; like dinner and a roof over her head.

She reached for her jacket and shrugged into it, as the elevation made the night air nippy even in early summer. Carefully locking the car doors, she went around to the trunk and opened it to remove her overnight case. Her bigger suitcases and swatch sample books could stay in there until she could decide what to do in the morning. Closing the trunk, she rummaged in her purse for the house key before picking up her bag and approaching the front door. At least she had managed to arrive before it was completely dark. With luck, there might be a note inside from the foreman regarding food. Preferably regarding the preparation and eating thereof! She looked over her shoulder before inserting the key in the big brass lock on the front door. There was a cluster of outbuildings down by the pasture; one of those might be a foreman's cottage. What was it the man at the junction had called him . . . Dodge? Yes, that was it . . . Jim Dodge.

She turned the key and opened the massive door easily, stepping inside to a slate entry hall. Depositing her overnight case on the polished green stone, she removed her key from the lock and dropped it carefully back in her handbag before letting the door shut behind her.

The long living room in front of her was just as magnificent as she had imagined it might be. Beige carpeting commenced at the edge of the slate and continued to the far wall. The same restful beige and oyster-white tones were repeated in the wall color and curtains flanking the windows along the front of the house. The monochromatic effect continued with creamy Lioz marble from Portugal used for facing the massive fireplace. Furniture provided the accents of color; two deep davenports patterned in brown, cinnamon, and burnt orange were in front of the fireplace and occasional chairs, picking up the same colors, were scattered throughout the big room. The tables and lamps were large, in keeping with the dimensions of the area, but artfully arranged. The total effect was of understated elegance and comfort.

"And I couldn't improve on it if I tried," she said suddenly, her voice sounding hushed in the vast room, "so I might as well find a place to bed down for the night and then get in touch with New York in the morning."

She was turning back to pick up her overnight bag when suddenly the living room was flooded with light as a tall figure appeared in a doorway at the far end of it.

"Good evening," he said politely, advancing toward her suddenly stricken form. "I hope I didn't frighten you but I wasn't expecting company."

Diana let out her breath slowly, conscious of the rapid pounding of her heart. "That's all right," she told him huskily, trying to steady her voice, "I didn't know there was anyone in the house to meet me."

She watched polite surprise register on his face. There was an almost imperceptible raising of eyebrows and she became aware of a piercing gaze from gray eyes behind the black-rimmed glasses perched on an aquiline nose.

"Was there supposed to be someone to meet you?"

"Well, of course." His patent disbelief trig-

27

gered impatience in her tone. "If you're Mr. Dodge, then surely . . ."

"But I'm not Mr. Dodge," he interrupted, "so I'm afraid you've made the wrong arrangements and gotten the wrong house. You'll find Mr. Dodge's place down the drive."

"I'm not looking for Mr. Dodge," she said in an equally icy tone, "or, at least, not in the way you seem to think I am. It's merely that Mrs. Robertson wired him when she sent me out here from New York. She knew that Dr. Reynolds wasn't at home so the foreman was the obvious one for me to contact."

"I see." The thin line of his mouth relaxed somewhat and his voice became a shade warmer. "It's too bad, but Mrs. Robertson had her facts wrong."

She raised her chin defiantly. "In what way?"

"She's behind times on her itinerary." He moved over to perch easily on the back of a couch and folded his arms. "I'm Matt Reynolds. Now . . . more to the point . . . who in the devil are you?"

Diana could only stare at the relaxed figure in stunned disbelief. This tall, good-looking man was miles away from her preconception of the absent-minded professor. There was no stoop nor frail figure; indeed, his shoulders looked broad and strong under the plaid wool shirt which topped casual khaki-colored trousers. His hair wasn't thinning and wispy; it was a healthy, sandy thatch cut short and starting to gray at the temples, which seemed just right for a man in his mid-thirties.

There was only one category where her mental picture had been correct; her professor had no time for intruders and this man's piercing gaze fitted the part exactly.

"If you could stop staring at me . . ." His words came out as if separated by a sharp knife, "I'd like to know who you are."

Diana came back to reality with an effort. "I'm . . . I'm your birthday present," she heard her voice babbling inanely.

His eyebrows climbed even higher in the sudden silence that followed.

"How nice of Aunt Violet," he said finally. "Last year, she just sent three neckties. Things are improving."

"Don't be ridiculous!" She was aware of the blush which had covered her cheeks. "I'm an interior decorator. Your aunt sent me out to redo your home as a birthday surprise."

He unfolded his arms and moved over to a chair. "It's a surprise all right, but it looks as if it will take a little more explaining. You'd better come over and sit down." He watched her move hesitantly forward and perch on the edge of a nearby chair. "Relax, I don't bite. You still haven't told me your name."

"Diana Burke." She chewed on her lower lip nervously. "I'm sorry to be so addled. You're quite a surprise to me too."

"So it would seem." He stretched long legs

out in front of him. "Whatever prompted Aunt Violet to hire a young girl like you?"

"I'm twenty-five, Dr. Reynolds."

"Is that so?" He took off his glasses and subjected her to the same searching scrutiny that he had encountered. His deliberate stare started at her wavy brown hair cut just longer than cap length, traveled down past brown eyes that were now looking at him defiantly, noted the short straight nose and the generous mouth compressed in a forbidding line. A second look encompassed her trimly fitting dress and passed down to admirable ankles.

"Wouldn't you like to take off your jacket?" he asked finally, shoving his glasses back on. "You must find it rather warm in here."

"No, thank you." She hugged it closer around her. "I think I'd better be going."

"Where?"

She looked down at her lap in sudden confusion. "Well . . . back to New York, I suppose."

His slight grin flashed. "It's a long trip for tonight. I'd hate to have Aunt Violet think I was so unreceptive to her generous present. No . . . sit down," he raised his hand authoritively as she started to rise in protest, "you'd better stick around. I can get in touch with my foreman tomorrow and we can track down my aunt's wire. Jim has been out on the high range getting the cattle moved for the past week. Western Union probably tried to contact him by phone down at his place and when they couldn't reach him, sent the message to his post office box in town."

"But why didn't your aunt wire you, instead?"

He shrugged slightly. "Because I was away in the Aleutians until this week. When I found I had all the information I needed on this particular research project, I came home to finish my report on it." There was a pause as he subjected her to another scrutiny through narrowed eyes. "You can't type, I suppose?" His tone was casual.

"You suppose wrong. Decorators are not exactly lilies of the field."

"I admit I don't know much about interior decorators," he drawled, giving the impression that such a lack of knowledge was not apt to bother him. "Do you have any shorthand?"

"Not really . . . just some squiggles that serve for note-taking." She frowned suddenly. "What's all this leading up to?"

He sat up straighter in his chair and adopted a businesslike tone. "Just this. My change of plans has resulted in a mixup all around. My secretary got married a few weeks ago and is taking an extended honeymoon for the summer months as I had planned to be up north until fall. Now I find I need someone to get my material into shape so that I can use it for presentation at a scientific congress this fall."

"But I have a job . . ."

"That's right and I'm it, just now," he said with some satisfaction. "Thanks to Aunt Violet."

"But I've been retained to decorate your house."

"That's just a formality," he said briskly. "You can think about redoing my study while you're typing in there. Since I won't dictate to you, you can decorate in the morning and type from my rough draft in the afternoon. In the meantime, maybe you can find something in the kitchen for our dinner tonight." He stood up and came over to stand in front of her. "You can cook, can't you?"

"Not really," she said again and stood up reluctantly. "Can't you?"

"Certainly . . . there's not much of a trick to it." He moved over to pick up her overnight case. "It's just that after a week, it would be nice to have a change of menu. Do you want to go up to your room now?"

"In a minute," she said absently. "What have you been eating?"

"Fish . . . all the time I was in Alaska," he said promptly. "Since I've been home, I've defrosted steak from the freezer. Thank God, the cook comes back from vacation the day after tomorrow."

She stared up at him. "You mean you've been eating steak for breakfast, lunch, and dinner?"

"There's nothing wrong with that menu other than getting a little dull after a week." He pulled his glasses off with one hand and poked them in a leather case in his shirt pocket. "The guest room is at the top of the stairs," he said politely. "Just follow me."

"What did you plan to do about your dinner tonight?" she persisted, following a few steps behind.

"I've got a steak thawing. Why?"

"One steak?"

"That's right," he said impatiently. "Why do you keep going on about it?"

"Maybe you haven't noticed," she said, catching him by the sleeve as he reached the foot of the stairs, "but there are now two of us."

The gray eyes looked down on her casually. "I've noticed. Don't worry, you won't have to go hungry. There is a perfectly good can opener and a pantry full of stuff."

Diana thought yearningly of the lunch she had missed. "Dr. Reynolds," she began.

"You needn't be so formal."

"Mr. Reynolds," she said deliberately, "my stomach is still on eastern daylight time which means I'm about to fall at your feet from malnutrition. You take my bag up and I'll find the kitchen."

"So you can cook as well," he said in a mild tone of pleased discovery.

"I can keep us alive until the cook returns," she corrected grimly.

"Blessings on Aunt Violet," he murmured, heading up the stairs.

"So it seems," she said fiercely, as she turned toward the kitchen wing. "I wonder why she didn't have me gift-wrapped!"

Chapter Two

By the time Diana was able to announce that dinner was ready, the actual onset of famine had been staved off by some judicious sampling that automatically becomes a privilege of the cook. The well-stocked pantry and refrigerator proved that Dr. Reynolds had stopped at the nearest supermarket on his way home and assembled more than the necessities even if he hadn't included the meat department on his shopping list. A wedge of cheese and some crackers together with a refreshing cup of tea had improved her disposition immeasurably, so when her host stuck his head around the door after disposing of her overnight bag and asked if there were anything he could do to help, she had waved him off politely without really taking her attention from the cookbook she had found in a convenient niche.

There had even been time to find attractive place mats for the oval breakfast table which was at the end of the big kitchen. She had considered candles and then discarded the idea, fearing that her new employer would consider it beyond her duties of cook and bottle washer. It was a pity though, because the green Irish linen mats and napkins provided a splendid background for the pale yellow dishes she had discovered in another cupboard and matching candles would have provided a fitting touch. Oh well, she thought defiantly as she unearthed the yellow tapers and put them in low holders, the most he could do was blow them out.

She carefully took her casserole dish out of the oven and placed it on a raffia mat in the center of the table, pulled off the severely practical white apron she had found on a handy hook and poked her head around the swinging door leading to the dining room. It was dark and deserted but there were low lamps turned on in the empty living room as she went in search of her host. Her feet slowed as they approached the closed door at the end of the room through which he had originally appeared. Should she stand in the living room and call or should she beard the lion in his den and knock on the door? She flipped a mental coin and had just raised her hand to knock when the door opened and he stood directly in front of her, absently stowing his glasses away in his shirt pocket.

"Oh!" It took a conscious effort on her part to keep her raised and clenched fist from rapping his broad chest.

He took in the situation quickly and moved easily to one side.

"You look like the Statue of Liberty," he said, flipping the light switch by the door. "Why didn't you call?"

Diana lowered her arm stiffly feeling all kinds of a fool. "This place is a little large for shouting."

"So it is." He took her elbow and moved her along beside him smartly. "I must show you the intercom and then you won't have to go chasing all over the place. Jill was responsible for having it installed."

"Your wife?" she asked evenly.

"My sister," he replied just as evenly, pushing open the swinging door to the kitchen and motioning for her to precede him. "She's visiting friends in Oregon right now. You'll meet her when she returns."

It was if a heavy weight had suddenly lifted from Diana's chest but she chose to ignore the implications just then.

"If I'm still here," she temporized.

He was equally casual. "That's right . . . if you're still here." He paused to admire the table. "Looks great." Then, leaning forward to survey the casserole, "Smells good, too. You light the candles and I'll see if I can find some wine to go with that Quiche Lorraine." He didn't miss the sudden stupefaction that flitted over her features. "Would you prefer a Moselle or a rose?"

"Er . . . it doesn't matter." She suddenly became aware that he was holding her chair and she dropped into it more rapidly than she would have chosen. Damn David Royle and his absurd fairy stories about absent-minded professors in the rugged wilderness! Damn . . . damn . . . damn!

"I looked in earlier to see if you'd like some sherry or a martini," Matt was saying as he eventually reappeared, bearing two sparkling Waterford wine glasses in one hand and an open green bottle in the other, "but you were industriously beating something and I didn't have the nerve to interrupt you." He poured carefully and put the glass before her. "Now, see if you like this."

She obediently sipped at the golden Rhine wine. "Lovely, it should be just right."

"We'll hope so," he said easily. "Let me serve you with our main course and you can do the honors with that green salad at your elbow. Don't tell me this other dish has creamed spinach?"

"It has creamed spinach," she told him wryly, watching him ladle out generous portions for both of them. "Dr. Reynolds, you don't really expect me to believe that you've existed here on steak for a week . . . not after seeing the contents of that refrigerator?"

"Miss Burke," he paused to pass her a warmed roll, "you don't really expect me to believe that you can't cook after tasting this feast, do you?" He seemed to enjoy the different expressions which were following each other over her face. "Let's just acknowledge we were both doing a little experimenting."

She chewed silently for a minute, staring down at her plate and then looked up to meet his quizzical gaze. Her lips twitched in an unwilling smile and then she lifted her wine glass in mock salute. "To the back of beyond," she said ruefully.

He looked puzzled and then amused. "Is that what they told you to expect?" He leaned back in his chair. "You aren't the first New Yorker who has come out here with candles in his suitcase."

"And there aren't any Indians?"

"Of course, there are Indians. I have Indian graduate students working on a special project this summer. There are others on the reservations. You'll also find Norwegians, Japanese, Lutherans, Episcopalians . . ."

"Don't spell it out," she said patiently. "I get the message."

He speared a mushroom carefully. "I thought you might. Any other misconceptions you'd like taken care of?"

"Is it true that you're a parasitologist?"

His stern mouth relaxed. "Quite true, unfortunately. Do you want to know about the paper you're going to be typing?"

She sighed. "I suppose I might as well."

"Such enthusiasm," he chided. "Roughly, it

has to do with tracing the life history of the liver fluke so it can be stopped before penetrating animal species."

Diana lowered her fork unconsciously. "Liver flukes?"

"Liver flukes," he confirmed.

The fork clattered onto her plate. "You've got the wrong body," she stated flatly. "What I don't know about liver flukes would fill volumes. And what's more," her voice rose defensively, "I don't want to know anything about them."

"Take it easy," he soothed, "and have some more wine. You're overtired."

"I'm not overtired . . . I'm just in the wrong place. I'm supposed to be in a little log cabin putting oilcloth on the table and instead I'm here . . ." she gestured forcefully . . . "using Balleek for a sugar and creamer because it goes better with the place mats than the Lenox in the next cupboard. Instead of tracing what kind of upholstery material you want for bunk bedspreads, I'm supposed to trace parasites on a typewriter. It's like coming into a movie in the middle of the second reel; I don't know what to do."

"If I could make a suggestion . . ." he put in smoothly.

"What?"

"Let's have some of that splendid lemon meringue pie I see cooling on the counter top and a cup of coffee."

She shook her head sorrowfully. "You haven't listened to a word I've been saying."

"I've listened," he corrected her, picking up his plate and taking it over to the sink, "the way I've listened to my sister and Aunt Violet for some years."

"And you're not impressed."

"I didn't say that."

She watched him clear the table efficiently without offering to help. He placed the pie in front of her with a silver server and put two dessert dishes at her elbow. The coffee was moved to his end of the table with the cups and saucers.

"You didn't say that," she went on, "but that's what you meant. You remind me of some impenetrable object; probably that's why your aunt sent me out here when she thought you weren't going to be around. You would have put the damper on her plan otherwise, wouldn't you?"

He poured the coffee and pushed her cup over to her. "You fuss too much, Miss Burke. There's no use going on about what might have happened; you've appeared at a providential time as far as I'm concerned, so let it rest at that. I don't expect you to become enamored with my research ideas. All you have to do is type reasonably well, spell so that the readers can determine the meaning," he took a bite of pie crust and chewed thoughtfully, ". . . and make a lemon meringue pie occasionally. That's all a decorative woman like you ever has to do."

To give Diana credit, she didn't choke on her pie or upset her coffee in his lap despite the temptation. It wasn't until they were leaving the room after the dishes were done that the kitchen door accidentally swung too freely and caught him a resounding whack between the shoulder blades almost propelling him into the hall. It was, quite possibly, the most satisfying thing that had happened since she left New York.

The next morning, she opened her eyes to look into a golden stream of sunlight which was spotlighting the head of her bed. She stared in bewilderment at the unfamiliar surroundings for a minute and then propped up on an elbow as her memory came flooding back. No wonder the off-white walls and beige rug seemed strange; there had been little time to be aware of them last night before she had fallen into bed and a deep sleep.

Now, as the morning sunlight came cheerfully through the sheer curtains, she could fully appreciate the charm of the suite in which Matthew Reynolds had installed her. Burnt orange accent color was used for the bedspread and the upholstery of the two occasional chairs. Diaphanous curtains went from ceiling to floor in panels of beige, oyster-white, pale yellow, and soft orange. Each blended easily into the companion shade and gave an over-all effect of brightness and gaiety. The same soft orange was picked up in the cushions of the chaise lounge under the windows.

Diana got up and located her slippers at the foot of her bed before padding into the adjoining bath. She paused to run a comb through her hair and then discovered she had left her shower cap in her overnight bag which was still on a luggage rack by the bed. Going back to the bedroom, she noticed the folded piece of paper which had been pushed partway under the closed outer door.

She stood motionless for a moment and then clenched her hands unconsciously. It was hardly apt to be a love note at this hour of the morning; it was far more likely to be a written notice of dismissal. Dr. Matthew Reynolds had accepted her apology for the swinging kitchen door with a notable lack of conviction and impassive demeanor. He had probably gone back to his study and decided that an impudent New York decorator-cum-typist was the last thing he needed in his austere existence and had written to tell her so.

The feeling of unhappiness that suddenly engulfed her was devastatingly new. She should be delighted at the thought of leaving Killara and all that it contained . . . especially its aloof and uncaring owner; delighted that he'd have to unearth a more willing typist from his erudite female colleagues. She should be completely thrilled and, to face it frankly, she wasn't.

Her slippered feet dragged as she approached the door and the folded piece of paper. She took it up gingerly and opened it. The firm handwriting blurred slightly before she could focus on it properly.

"Miss Burke," it began in peremptory fashion. "Sorry to seem inhospitable but an urgent problem has come up in my research lab which I must handle. I hope to be home by late afternoon but my foreman, Jim Dodge, will be waiting to show you around the grounds when it's convenient for you. You can contact him on the house phone. Matt Reynolds." The signature at the bottom of the note was as decisive as the man himself.

So she was to be let off for her idiotic lapse with the swinging door. An inner voice warned that Dr. Reynolds might overlook one such escapade but that it wouldn't be wise to try for two. At any rate, she was home free for the moment; the sun was shining and the world was waiting to be conquered after some toast and coffee.

She found the latter being kept warm in an electric percolater when she descended to the kitchen after a quick shower. The room was still in the immaculate condition it had been left in the previous night. Either the master of the house had been trained to wash his breakfast dishes or he had made do with some coffee in a disposable cup.

Ordinarily toast and coffee was Diana's

standard morning fare but she weakened on seeing the provisions in the refrigerator and was just finishing her scrambled egg when a tall figure knocked at the back door and then pushed it ajar.

"Good morning!" His drawl was straight from the television commercials featuring rangy cowboys.

"Good morning," she said, pushing back her chair and standing to greet him. "You must be Mr. Dodge."

"That's right, ma'am. The boss said you'd be wanting to take a look around the place this morning . . . that is, if you're Miss Burke."

"Diana Burke. And I would appreciate having a short tour if you have the time."

There was a barely perceptible hesitation before a grin flashed over his tanned face. "I'll just make the time, ma'am," he said in that pleasant drawl.

She melted immediately. Now there was a Westerner who looked the way one was supposed to look. He was big and broad-shouldered with blond hair worn long enough to be sun-streaked on top. The denim pants and jacket which fitted snugly were clean but worn and his feet looked enormous in intricately designed black cowboy boots. A grimy white hat with a wide brim was clutched at his side. His age was difficult to estimate but probably was in the early thirties.

His sharp blue eyes surveyed her quickly.

"The boss told me to keep an eye out for some signs of life in the kitchen as he didn't know what time you'd be stirring."

"Then you saw Dr. Reynolds this morning?"

"Sure did, ma'am. He was down at my place just past six. He must have seen the lights when I got home late last night."

"And you received the wire from Mrs. Robertson about my arrival?" she asked.

"I collected it down at the post box yesterday," he said. "Hope it didn't inconvenience you that I wasn't here when you came."

"Not at all," she lied politely, rinsing out her coffee cup and running water over her plate in the sink. "Oh, I'm sorry . . . would you like a cup of coffee?"

"No thank you, ma'am. The boss and I had breakfast down at my place."

So Matt Reynolds had gone out for breakfast, after all. If that was the case, he had gone beyond the duty of a considerate host in making coffee just for her.

"If you're ready . . ." The foreman opened the door suggestively.

"Will I need a sweater?" she asked, looking down at her matching blue wool shirt and slacks.

He appeared to consider. "No ma'am, I don't think so. We'll just make it a point to stay in the sun."

"All right." She accompanied him out onto a

45

flagged terrace by the back door. "This seems to be an awfully big place to keep up with so little help."

He paused in midstride. "You must have gotten the wrong idea. There's plenty of help around most of the time. You just caught us at change-overs and vacations. The cook's been on holiday and she'll be back tomorrow. She brings her niece with her to help out with the housework. The reason it's so deserted out here," he gestured toward the outbuildings, "is that my men have taken the cattle up to the high range for the summer."

"I see." She surveyed the two fenced pastures which were beyond the kitchen-garden area. Two horses were grazing at the far end, while closer to the first fence a small burro of mottled gray raised a curious head as they approached. "I didn't know there were cattle on the ranch, as well."

Her companion let out a guffaw of laughter. "Why, the cattle are what Killara's famous for! The Reynolds family runs the finest beef in this part of the country. You won't see them at this time of year, though . . . they won't be comin' down again 'til about September."

She looked over at him with a puzzled expression as they came up to the split-rail fence. "Why do you need to have men with them all the time?"

"Plenty of reasons . . . to put out the salt, keep the herd scattered, and make sure that

46

none of the folks get any ideas about poaching."

"Do people do that?"

He was gentle with her obvious lack of knowledge. "They sure do with that much money walking around on the hoof. Besides that, the boys can ride herd and make sure the cattle don't start coming back down too early in the season."

"But how does Dr. Reynolds find time for cattle? I thought he spent most of his time at scientific research?"

"He does." Dodge leaned against the fence. "He hires people like me to run the ranching part."

"Oh . . ." her tone was dry. "An absentee landlord."

He shook his head and then realized that he was still carrying his hat and clapped it on his head. "No sirree, Matt Reynolds can ride fence with the best of 'em. That's why he quit working fulltime at the university; he didn't want to be so far away from Killara. Then, a couple of years ago, they got some federal grant or something and started a special research laboratory down here on the Sound. He usually has a handful of graduate students working there on special projects for their doctorates. Folks come from all over to work with them. Beats me what they find to look at in a bunch of bugs." He reached for a cigarette from the package in his shirt pocket and offered one to her.

"No thank you, not right now." She smiled

up at him. "I really didn't know much about Dr. Reynolds or Killara until I came here. His aunt didn't bother with explanations."

"That Mrs. Robertson in New York . . ." his tone was scornful. "I've heard Miss Jill tell about her. Seems to think she's got more money than sense."

Diana sought to change the subject. "Dr. Reynolds mentioned that he'd be back tonight."

"That's what he told me, too." The foreman was easily diverted. "He has to finish some project in the next month or so . . . then he can be gone this fall. Miss Jill said he'd accepted a visiting lecturer's post back East. Before then, he'll be busy helping to bring the cattle down."

"Are the cattle up in the mountains around here?" Diana asked, nodding toward the hills ringing the plateau.

"Quite a ways beyond," Dodge said, flicking the ash from his cigarette. "Most of the land around here is kept for timber rights. The cattle are in higher country."

"What are the outbuildings down there?" She pointed toward the white-painted structures she had noted on her arrival the night before.

"That first one is the garage. If you'll give me your keys, I'll move your car down to it later."

"Thank you very much . . . you'll find an

extra set of car keys in the glove compartment and I'll unlock it as soon as I get back to the house." She put her hands in her slack pockets as the air was still chilly even in the sun. "What's the building beyond the garage?"

"That's a machinery storage shed and the bunk house is at the far end. That's where the boss spent the night." He paused and gazed at her questioningly through narrowed eyes, then went on without acknowledging her involuntary look of surprise. "My diggings are in that separate house beyond." He pointed to a steep-roofed cottage at the end of the drive. "The barn takes care of all the livestock they keep up here." He gestured toward the two bay horses cropping grass at the far end of the meadow. "There's a stream past that last fence to furnish all the water we need . . . it comes from a spring halfway up the mountains."

"It's a beautiful spot." She looked at the rich brown coats of the grazing animals. "How did those horses happen to get left behind?" She was carrying on the conversation with an effort as her mind was still sorting out the implications of Matthew Reynolds' sudden desertion to the bunkhouse the previous night. It was difficult to fathom his reasons—probably it was an oddly old-fashioned gesture in a world that had almost forgotten such niceties of behavior.

"They're a pair of mighty fine trail horses," Dodge was answering, "and they belong to the boss's sister. Miss Jill calls them Dee and Dum."

"Doesn't Dr. Reynolds ride?"

His low chuckle boomed out again. "He sure does, though he doesn't set as much store by horses as his sister. His palomino is in the barn this morning."

"Oh look, that cute burro is coming this way." She reached her hand through the fence to pat the rough nose of the sturdy but scruffy little animal that was coming straight toward them.

"Get back, ma'am!" Dodge took her by the shoulders and pushed her away from the fence hurriedly. "That little devil would rather have a bite of you for breakfast than all the oats in the manger."

Diana stared in bewilderment at the watery blue eyes now regarding her steadily at close range.

"I didn't know," she faltered. "Why do they keep her if she's so dangerous?"

"Carmen isn't dangerous exactly . . ."

"Carmen?" Her voice rose in disbelief.

"That's what Matt calls her because she's a Spanish burro," he said in a resigned tone. "The only human being Carmen really likes is the boss and he lets her have the run of the pasture. She used to be a pack animal 'til she hurt her hoof." He pointed to the burro's left foreleg where the hoof was growing in a slight malformation. "Now that she's not working, her disposition is worse than ever. I keep asking the boss to take some of the cussedness out of her, but it's no dice."

As if she knew she were the object of their conversation Carmen, at that juncture, merely snorted through her velvety nostrils and twitched her tail impatiently.

"I'm sorry I didn't bring you something," Diana told her soothingly. "Next time, I'll see whether you prefer carrots or sugar."

"Next time, you might be minus a thumb," Dodge said. "You know anything about horses?"

"Not much," she told him cheerfully, "and less about burros. They didn't have any of those on the bridle paths in Central Park."

"If I didn't have to get back up to the cattle, I'd give you a lesson or two."

"I think I'll read an instruction book first," she said laughing. "Don't worry, any jaunts I take for now will be on foot. I would like to go for a walk this afternoon while I'm waiting for Dr. Reynolds to come home. Is there a special path?"

"There are quite a few," he said guardedly, "but I think you'd better stick close to the house 'til you've got some company. Some of the trails aren't very well marked. The boss said you were to make yourself at home and he'd talk over any of your decorating schemes when he got back. That might be safer for now." He glanced at his watch. "If you'll excuse me, Miss

Burke, I'd better get going. I've got a mess of things waiting to be done before I get back up to the range."

"Is there anything I can do to help?"

"No thank you, ma'am." His nice smile flashed again in his lined face. "I'm sorry I can't stay around and introduce you to places properly. Maybe when I get things under control, I can drive you down to the settlement on the Sound or up to Vancouver some night for dinner. I understand that you're going to be here for quite a while." His voice took on a warmer note. "It will be mighty nice to have a little feminine company close by."

"Thank you." Despite her best intentions, a tinge of amusement crept into Diana's tone. Mr. Dodge was entirely too efficient when it came to the opposite sex; the blithe assurance in his invitation spoke of successful forays before. "We'll have to see what develops," she said casually. "I haven't really had a chance to talk to Dr. Reynolds about my job here. By the time dinner was over last night, I was too sleepy to do anything other than fall into bed."

"That's what he said." Dodge's remark left Diana with the impression that Matt Reynolds' references to her social behavior of the night before had been scanty and hardly complimentary. "He thought you'd probably appreciate a chance to get rested today while he's away."

"How thoughtful of him," she purred in a way that indicated nothing of the sort. "I'll get back to the house then and let you go on with your work. We won't see you tonight?"

He chose to interpret her query as personal rather than informational and beamed in a self-satisfied way. "No, not tonight, ma'am. I'll be back up with my men, but I plan to be down in a day or so and we'll arrange something then." He leaned forward to give her shoulder an intimate squeeze and in doing so, came within reach of Carmen's long muzzle. Instantly, her mouth opened to reveal yellowed teeth which fastened with gusto on Dodge's sleeve.

"Why you no-good . . . jackass!" The foreman pulled back immediately with a ripping of cloth. He swallowed the rest of the epithet in deference to Diana who was doing her best to stifle her laughter. "You see what I mean about getting too close, ma'am," he said, giving the stoic burro a withering look.

"I see what you mean," she said with a straight face. "Thanks for the tour. I'll get back to the house now and wash my breakfast dishes. See you soon." She turned and walked rapidly back to the main house, pausing only when she had reached the back door to look over her shoulder. Jim was disappearing into the machine shed without a backward glance. "One up for Carmen," she murmured, closing the kitchen door behind her. Of the two possible menaces, she thought she preferred facing the one with four legs; six feet of amorous cowboy would be harder to handle. At least, she had no worries on that score with Matt Reynolds; he had wasted no time in avoiding a compromising situation. "I wish I knew whether he was protecting his reputation or mine," she muttered, turning on the hot water in the sink with a twist that made the pipes protest. "Somehow, I have a feeling it was both."

By stretching out the cleaning of the kitchen and then unpacking and tidying in her bedroom, she succeeded in occupying an hour and a half. She was loath to peer into the other bedrooms of the house without direct orders; so she merely straightened chairs in the living room, dusted a few table tops, and then peeked into Matthew Reynolds' study.

It was a paneled room with bookshelves along one wall and a red brick fireplace which shared a chimney with its counterpart in the living room. Deep green leather chairs with matching ottomans were placed next to convenient reading lamps and, by the windows, a long kneehole desk was covered with a profusion of papers and reference books. A typewriter was nearby on a movable metal typing table. She could well imagine Dr. Reynolds' horror of feminine fripperies or color accents being added to this room. Even the Navajo rugs on the polished floors carried out the browns and greens of the paneling and the furniture. And from the untidy look of the desk, he would take an equally dim view of anyone trying to straighten his effects.

Diana looked at her wrist watch again. It was barely noon and certainly too nice a day to think of sitting around inside. Surely Jim Dodge would be on his way by now and there would be no one to keep her from taking a picnic lunch and enjoying it by the side of the stream she had seen in the distance.

As a concession to the occasion, she changed from the loafers she was wearing to sturdy walking shoes and put a bright yellow cardigan around her shoulders. She then dug around in the cabinet under the kitchen sink and found a brown paper bag to carry the bologna sandwich she had hastily put together. There was a moment of indecision when she weighed the merits of hot coffee over the disadvantage of having to carry a thermos, and the coffee lost. In its place she substituted a can of root beer she found on a bottom shelf of the refrigerator.

In the process of going out the door, she paused to write a note on the pad clipped to a corner cupboard. "Gone for a walk by the creek," she wrote quickly, "Back this afternoon" and signed her name. After all, she had no way of knowing when her host would return, and it was common courtesy to let him know of her whereabouts if he should get back earlier than he expected.

She skirted the pasture fence, giving Carmen and the two mares a wide berth. Her relations with horses had been limited, to say the least, and she wasn't sure if Jill Reynolds would care for strangers interfering in any way with her expensive livestock. The designation of trail horse was new to her but the two occupants of the pasture were sleek and lovely, whatever their pedigree. Either she should have attended more horse shows, she decided, or asked Jim Dodge what a trail horse was.

She put back her head and inhaled deeply, filling her lungs with the fresh mountain air. It was wonderful to be in such a glorious place! The sun was shining on the green grass, the snow-capped peaks were providing an awe-inspiring frame for the smaller mountains in front of them and the tall stands of Douglas fir, hemlock, and an occasional cedar tree were stalwart guardians on the steep hillsides around her. It would be fun to wander up the stream after lunch and see what other types of timber grew in this corner of the country.

A convenient flat rock by the creekside provided a table for her sandwich and cold drink. After eating, she merely stretched out on the big, smooth surface, as indolent as a tabby cat reclining on a sunny carpet. The only sounds were the occasional chatter of a bird or the rustle of its wings and the gurgle of the shallow creek as it flowed around a steppingstone crossing which someone from Killara probably had designed. The peace—the almost uncanny silence—caused her to relax still further and, pillowing her head on her arm, to drop into an unscheduled nap.

A guilty conscience must have disturbed her later because she hurriedly sat up, grimacing at the stiffness of her bones in the process. Flat rocks, however sunny, could benefit from an air mattress if they were used for a bed. Her watch had stopped at noon simply because she had neglected to wind it. However, there should still be time for a stroll, she decided, as the sun was threading a latticework of light through the trees even though it was not as high as before.

She folded her brown paper bag carefully and put it in her pocket. Then she flattened her soft drink can and used the edge of it to dig a shallow hole in which she could bury it. She scuffed the dirt back in and succeeded in leaving the halcyon spot just as she had found it.

There was a narrow trail to follow which wound upward along the creek bank, carpeted and padded by the fir and hemlock needles which had fallen over the years. As long as she stayed on the track or used the creek as a guide, there was little chance of getting lost. The thought of such a happening made her pause for a moment. It would almost be worth staging just to see if Matt Reynolds' aplomb could be upset by anything. Even a swinging door hadn't disconcerted him for long.

She climbed onward and upward steadily, noting that she was still seeing hemlock groves but now they were interspersed with alder near the side of the creek. At one point, she had to duck to avoid the spines of a huge devil's club growing by the edge of the trail.

The current of the stream increased with the steepness of the climb and the splashing of the water became louder. At one point, she paused to rest in a clearing of bright green vine maples. Nearby there was a bank of smooth glacial pebbles just asking to be lobbed into the fast-moving water. Childish occupations please childish minds, she decided, and selected a handful of pebbles to throw.

Suddenly she became conscious of another roar of water above the noise of the stream and she strolled up the trail to see a long waterfall cascading down over rocks on the sheer mountainside to end in feathery spray at the brook. Shakespeare's lines from *As You Like It* flashed through her mind . . . "And this our life, exempt from public haunt, finds tongues in trees, books in the running brooks, sermons in stones, and good in everything."

"I didn't realize before just what he meant," she murmured in a reverent whisper.

It was when she was reluctantly swinging around to start on her way back down the path that she saw the cabin. The weathered cedar shakes of the steep A-frame roof settled so gently among the trees that it might have grown there with them. Then she noticed the narrow footpath which led from the main trail up to the slight elevation on which it was located. Still curious, she walked cautiously up the winding path, stopping some twenty feet from the back of the structure.

"Hello," she called out hesitantly, loath to trespass on someone's private domain. "Anyone home?"

Silence greeted her words, the muted sound of the waterfall behind her the only disturbance in the atmosphere. Still she hesitated, feeling uneasy for no explicable reason. Then, mentally giving herself a push, she went on . . . brushing past the clumps of Oregon grape and salal which grew by the back of the windowless cabin. The path circled around and she found herself at a wooden front step and a weathered door standing ajar. She stood there quietly and looked around the slight cleared area in front of the cabin. Fifty feet away was the beginning of a spacious corral enclosed by the same type of split-rail fencing which bordered the pastures of Killara; probably this was part of the Reynolds property. Her sense of intruding lightened and she moved forward to widen the crack of the cabin door and step into the shelter.

A room almost totally devoid of furnishings, other than four unadorned walls and a rough stone fireplace, greeted her. Two sturdy shelves extended from either side of the big chimney with a dusty kerosene lamp standing atop one and a well-worn sleeping bag abandoned in the corner of the other. A narrow bentwood rocker with a sagging seat was pushed carelessly in front of the fireplace while on a wooden table in the corner some kitchen oddments were scattered aimlessly.

Hardly a home away from home, she mused, and leaned absently against the front of the fireplace to inspect the log mantel. Then suddenly she knelt and peered into the fireplace ashes.

"I'll be darned," she said softly, "I'm not the only visitor. Somebody's had a fire here just a few minutes ago."

As she started to rise, the light in the cabin was extinguished almost simultaneously with the noise of the door closing. Panic-stricken, she stumbled across the darkened room to fumble for the wooden handle of the door and pull at it frantically. There wasn't a lock so it must have gotten jammed when caught by the wind. After tugging ineffectually and then beating on the door panel with her fist in frustration, she let her hand fall limply to her side. A sudden realization kept her motionless. That door may have gotten jammed shut but not by an act of nature; there hadn't been a breath of wind all afternoon. The door had been slammed by someone determined to imprison her for an unknown reason.

She shivered involuntarily and stood back. The cabin walls had either become her prison or her fortress; only time would tell. In the meantime, all she could do was wait.

Chapter Three

It was difficult to determine the passage of time in the hours that followed. The closing of the door meant that the only light which could filter into the cabin must come from the two ventilators up near the peak of the steep roof. As they were obviously for the passage of fresh air rather than illumination, she soon decided that it would be necessary to light the kerosene lamp. She took it down and stared at it dubiously. Fortunately, it had been recently filled so she lowered the wick carefully and then set it aglow with a match from the top of the kitchen table. The chimney of the lamp was dusty so she blew on it and stepped back hurriedly as the cloud of dust particles settled around her. She waited for them to subside and then put the glass top on the lamp, turning down the wick meanwhile to keep the black smoke at a minimum.

The warm glow of yellow lamplight lifted her spirits immediately. In the new hopeful mood, she walked back to the door and tugged at it again but it remained as immobile as before. She put her ear to the panel and strained to hear any outside noises but an unbroken silence still surrounded and invaded the cabin.

Resolutely she straightened and turned back to survey the interior of her prison. This time she noticed a small pile of split firewood and kindling spilled at the end of the stone hearth. If lamplight was helpful, a fireplace fire would be a real morale booster.

There was no paper but she found a sharp knife on the table in the odds and ends of kitchen flatware and she was able to splinter and feather the kindling wood. Carefully she put the flame of a match under the little shavings of wood and held her breath until the fire caught. "Thank heaven for Girl Scout training," she breathed exultantly, and fed the growing flames until they could catch on the bigger logs. Once the fire was safely ablaze, she pulled the tired rocking chair directly in front of the fireplace and sat in it, basking in the newfound warmth. She was comfortable for the moment, at least, although it would have been nice if she could have unearthed a T-bone steak behind the firewood. Her picnic lunch had been spartan and its effects had long since worn off. She bit her lower lip in sudden frustration; there wasn't a chance of anyone looking for her until Matt Reynolds returned home and happened to find her note in the kitchen. Jim Dodge would be up at his range camp by this time and unavailable for any searching efforts. She thought of his earnest attempt to keep her by the house when she had talked to him and wished desperately that she had followed his instructions. Evidently he was experienced in nursing greenhorns. By the time Matt Reynolds found her, and she was careful to avoid an *if* in her thinking, he would be ready to send her packing without further discussion.

She hugged her arms over her breast, wishing that she had put on something warmer than a cardigan sweater over her shirt. But then, she really should be looking at the cheerful side of things. Whoever had decided to imprison her evidently was going to remain anonymous; possibly she had surprised some passerby who had been using the cabin for a clandestine drinking bout. She looked at the barren surroundings again; no one in his right mind would pick such an uncomfortable place for anything else. At any rate, it was better that they had chosen to escape rather than attempt to join her. The shiver that suddenly coursed through her body was not entirely caused by the draft of cold air behind her. Resolutely, she put a mental block on any further imaginative thinking and concentrated grimly on her dwindling pile of firewood.

It was down to the last log when she heard a noise outside and grew rigid with fright. There was a sudden clank of metal, then heavy footsteps on the porch and before she could do more than utter a small terror-stricken gasp the door flew open and a tall figure strode in.

"What in the devil are you waiting for," Matt Reynolds asked in clipped, angry tones, ". . . rescue by the Marines?"

"Ohhh." Relief washed through her body and caused her to sag back into the chair.

"It's a good thing you had sense enough to build a fire," he went on, the anger evident in his grim expression. "I was just about to turn back when I smelled smoke and realized you might have holed up in here." He pulled off his heavy plaid mackinaw and put it on a hook by the door, then stood beside it clad in a wool shirt and khaki pants. "At least you used your head in some ways."

"I didn't think about using the fire for a signal," she confessed in a hesitant tone, "I was just using it to keep warm."

He shot a look at the last log. "And what were you going to do after that was gone?"

"I don't know," she said in a meek voice. "Stop barking at me, for heaven's sake. I'm so glad to see you I could cry. I don't know how you opened the door but at least you got in . . ."

"What do you mean?" he growled. "I opened the door by pushing on it. There's nothing complicated about that. What I can't understand . . ." and he finally unbent enough to stride forward and glower down at her, "what I can't understand is what you're doing here in the first place. I've been searching up and down the creek trail." He shot a quick glance over her. "You're not hurt, are you?"

"No . . . not in the way you mean." Confusion made her hesitate and then rush on. "I couldn't walk out."

"For lord's sake, why not?"

"I'm telling you"—her hands were clenched at her side—"that the door was locked." The way his eyebrows started to rise caused her voice to rise as well. "Or if it wasn't locked, it was blocked or stuck together by leprechauns or something. Do you think I'd be sitting in here freezing and starving if I had any alternative?"

He raked impatient fingers through his hair and stared at her with a peculiar expression. "Okay, Miss Burke . . . calm down. We've each had a turn at losing our temper. Now, I'd better do something about making this place a little more comfortable for an overnight stop."

"Don't tell me we have to spend the night here?" Her relief at being rescued was submerged in a sudden desire to see the last of the chilly room.

"I'm not thrilled about it myself but if you'll take a look out the door you'll see that it's dark outside and Bob doesn't come equipped with headlights."

"Bob?"

"My horse," he said with exaggerated patience. "I'd better go out and turn him into the corral."

"Can't I come?"

"Look . . ." for the first time his voice softened, "I'll be right back. You can wait in the doorway if you want."

"All right." Her laugh was tremulous as she followed him. "I don't mean to be an idiot but . . ."

"Then stop acting like one and grab onto some of the stuff I've got here." He pulled a saddle bag off the buckskin-colored horse that was standing unconcernedly cropping grass by the porch with his braided rein dragging on the ground. "Take that inside . . . here, pile this blanket roll on top of it."

She did as he ordered, putting the saddle bag over the seat of the chair and piling the rolled blanket on top of it. Eventually Matt came in carrying his saddle and blanket to drop them on the floor by the door.

"Do you need any more help?" she asked hesitantly.

He shook his head. "There's nothing else to do. I'll turn Bob into the corral and check if there's any firewood left at the side of the cabin. You can dive into those saddle bags and see if there's anything there that appeals to you." He was gone before she could answer, leaving the door carefully ajar behind him.

She opened the stiff leather pockets and pulled out a packet of thick sandwiches. There was a silver flask of . . . she sniffed carefully . . . of brandy and another flat flask of coffee, hot and marvelously fragrant. They should bottle that lovely smell and sell it by the ounce, she decided. Deliberately, she put the food atop the mantel and waited for Matt Reynolds to reappear.

He did in a very few minutes with a bridle looped over his shoulder and carrying four pieces of firewood. He shrugged the bridle off onto the saddle gear and then strode over to the hearth and dropped the logs at the end of it.

"Cherish them," he said in a disgusted tone, "because that's the entire wood supply. I'd like to get my hands on the so-and-so who has depleted our store."

"You mean the woodpile is missing?"

"I mean just that. This cabin isn't used during the winter months but we leave it open in case anyone needs shelter during the snow season. There's always a pile of firewood left and it's an unwritten law out here that you replace any wood that you use."

"Then I wasn't imagining things," she said in a strangely quiet tone. "There *was* someone who barred the door."

He gave her a frowning glance. "Are you sure of that?"

"No . . . not really. I couldn't be sure because I didn't see or hear anyone but how else could that door have gotten barred? The only thing that could have happened was that someone shoved a piece of wood or some obstruction through the outside handle. Later, they must have removed it. After the first hour, I didn't go near the door to test it . . . there didn't seem to be any use."

He nodded absently, piling wood on the fire and coaxing it back into life. "There may be something in what you say, considering the depleted wood supply. It seems someone has been using this place fairly regularly."

"And that's another thing," she said excitedly. "Someone had built a fire just before I came on the scene because there were still hot coals in the ashes."

"It looks as if you flushed a trespasser. He probably decided to keep you incarcerated for a while to discourage you from coming again. He couldn't have known you were staying at Killara and thought you were just a hiker." Matt stood erect and brushed at his hands. "If you'd like to wash before eating, there's a flashlight over there to guide you down to the stream." He looked down at her with a serious expression. "Or do you feel nervous about wandering around alone?"

She shook her head and went over by the saddle to get the flashlight. "Not now. The only thing I feel nervous about at this point is that you might eat the sandwiches while I'm gone."

A crooked grin softened his features. "I promise to save you a bite, but only if you hurry."

The icy water of the stream proved a wonderful astringent for her hands and face. She tried to pat her tousled hair into some sort of order as she climbed back up to the cabin. Next time, she wouldn't venture off the ranch without a comb in one pocket, a mirror in the other, and a piece of beef jerky in her hand!

The lamplight provided a soft welcome through the half-open door. At the other end of the room, Matt had pulled the sleeping bag down from the shelf and arranged it as a rough cushion on the floor, using the blanket roll and two of the bigger pieces of firewood as a back.

"Look who's making like a Boy Scout now," she praised.

"When faced with an emergency . . . make do with the materials at hand," he quoted solemnly. "One of the important rules of the outdoors. You'd better take the rocker . . . it will be more comfortable."

"No thanks." She sank wearily onto the makeshift floor cushion. "I spent far too long in that darned chair."

He handed a sandwich to her. "Want to start with this or would you rather revive with some brandy first?"

She shook her head. "Not on an empty stomach."

"Haven't you had any food?"

"Not since lunch." She enumerated her sparse picnic menu. "So you can see why I was about to start chewing on the kindling."

"No candy bars or dried fruit in your pockets?"

She took a healthy bite of her sandwich before shaking her head. "I forgot. Besides, I wasn't planning on a safari."

"Forgetting is no excuse when you're hiking in this country," he told her sternly. "Any number of things could happen so that some extra food would be handy."

"I know, teacher," she said meekly, and then apologized as his eyes narrowed in reproof. "Pay no attention to me. I'm so happy to see you and your cheese sandwiches that I could sing the 'Hallelujah Chorus.'"

"Well don't! I'll go down and wash those two cups on the table so we'll have something for our coffee." He smiled reassuringly as he noted her anxious expression. "Relax, I'll be right back. Besides . . . think of the chance I'm taking leaving you alone with the last sandwich."

When he had returned and the coffee was poured, she insisted that he eat that last sandwich.

"No thanks, I had something to eat before I left the house," he assured her. "We'll save it. You might fancy a sandwich for breakfast rather than the chocolate bars I have in my jacket pocket."

She swallowed her last bite of sandwich with an audible effort. "Are you sure we can't get back to Killara tonight?" she asked hesitantly.

"Not unless you happen to have a couple of

spotlights with you," he said casually. "There isn't any moonlight and I don't fancy riding double down that trail when it's as black as the inside of a hat. We can leave in the morning as soon as it's light. Now, will you have some brandy?"

She darted a quick glance at his face to see if there had been a double meaning in his last remark, but found his expression as impenetrably bland as before.

"I don't think so, thanks," she told him.

He poured a dollop of brandy into his coffee. "Sure? It might warm you a bit. When that firewood goes, I'm afraid it's apt to get chilly in here."

She raised an eyebrow. "And there's no way to escape that?"

"Well . . . we should survive." He put his coffee cup on the floor beside him while he fished in his pocket for a cigarette. "Would you like one?"

"Yes, please." She leaned forward to accept a light. "I'm not worried about surviving; what's the social etiquette for unplanned overnight stays in the woods? Do we huddle on the hearth watching the warm coals die?"

"I think it would be more practical to roll out that sleeping bag of mine that you're sitting on. Fortunately, it's double-size so it shouldn't be too bad. What a pity I didn't leave an air mattress behind, as well."

"You must be kidding," she breathed.

"I'm certainly not. That floor will be mighty hard before morning, and an air mattress would be an improvement."

"I meant kidding about sharing that sleeping bag," she said indignantly, sitting bolt upright. "I can manage to be quite comfortable in the chair, thank you." Her voice wasn't as assured as she hoped, remembering the sheer torture of that sagging, broken reed seat earlier in the day.

"Oh, for lord's . . ." he broke off in the middle of his epithet and subdued his temper with an effort. "Well, it's your decision," he said finally, standing up and putting his empty coffee cup on the mantel before throwing his unfinished cigarette in the fire. "I'll give you the blanket for extra warmth."

"All right." She stood beside him. "Are you going to . . ." She hesitated over her choice of words.

"I am now going to bed," he said distinctly, as if addressing a slow learner. "Since I don't plan to remove anything except my boots, you needn't turn poppy-red and start stammering. Here," he tossed her the blanket and then set about unrolling the big sleeping bag. Finally, he went over to take two chocolate bars from his jacket pocket and put them on the table before rolling the coat and putting it down at the top of his bag to serve as a makeshift pillow. "Do you want the lamp for anything else?"

She shook her head and watched, wide-eyed,

as he blew it out and then put the remaining pieces of wood on the fire causing it to flare into renewed warmth.

"Better enjoy it while you can," he told her as he sat down on the edge of his sleeping bag and pulled off his serviceable brown riding boots which extended just above his ankle. He placed the pair neatly side by side at the end of the hearth and then slid inside the wide zippered bag, pulling the rolled jacket more comfortably under his head. "If you should want to change your mind when the fire dies down, you'd better come along in here with me. Don't be a little fool and freeze there for the rest of the night. If you're worried about conventions, you can stuff the blanket between us, but, frankly, I think you'd do better to use it for a pillow. And if you're worried about any flaming romantic ideas," his voice sounded hatefully amused, "I assure you that a sleeping bag without an air mattress leaves a lot to be desired in that line."

"I am not worried about your flaming romantic ideas," she said in a choked tone.

"I don't know whether to be glad about that or disappointed," he said, settling more comfortably on his side. "At any rate, you're quite safe. Tonight's schedule does not include the deflowering of any maidens, so I suggest you get some sleep. That's what I intend to do."

And as she watched in offended silence, he proceeded to do just that.

The time dragged by in interminable fashion. As the last logs burned away, she discovered that she was looking at her reset and rewound watch on the average of every three minutes. The chair seat had long since taken on the aspect of an oriental torture device and finding a comfortable way to lounge on a narrow, armless piece of furniture was utterly impossible.

Once again, she directed an uncertain look at the sleeping figure a few feet away. Matt Reynolds' even breathing and relaxed body proved that he wasn't suffering in the least.

Diana yawned enormously and twisted again in the miserable chair. Now that the fire was dying down, the cold drafts at her back felt as if they were down from the Arctic ice cap. Trying to stay wrapped in a blanket cocoon was a splendid idea but completely impractical. She looked again at the recumbent figure on the floor. That miserable man! As the red coals in the fireplace gave a last defiant sputter, she stood up stiffly.

"If you can't fight 'em . . . join 'em," she muttered, pulling the blanket from her shoulders and folding it swiftly into a lumpy square. She laid the blanket at the top of the sleeping bag as far as possible from Matt's sleeping figure. The heck with conventions if it meant waking up with a stiff neck! Thank heaven it was a double bag. Lord knows what she would have done if it had been a single one. Probably, she acknowledged ruefully, she'd have gotten in just the same.

She pulled off her shoes and put them within arm's reach before stealthily snaking down into the warm bag. The cocoon of warm air felt blissful after the last hour on that confounded chair. She snuggled happily into the blanket pillow under her head.

"I'm glad you finally decided to be sensible," came Matt's voice from the other side. "Now we can get some sleep. Good night." And he turned his back to her deliberately, edging as far toward his side of the bag as possible.

Diana caught her breath in sudden chagrin. Didn't the man miss anything? She exhaled slowly and then yawned, despite herself. It was too late to play games. When she fell asleep, she was still thinking that he needn't have been so pointed in his complete and utter lack of interest.

The thin light of dawn was just filtering through the ventilators at the cabin's ridgepole when Matt opened his eyes some hours later. He stirred restlessly and felt his bones creak in protest at the hard floor beneath them. All at once he became aware of the sleeping bag and his immediate surroundings.

"Lord," he thought muzzily, "I'm too old for this camping stuff . . . I'll be stiff for a week." He turned his head warily, suddenly remembering Diana's midnight capitulation into the warmth and comparative comfort of the sleeping bag. Then he discovered a feminine head pleasantly nuzzling into the crook of his shoulder and a slight curved figure close to his side. Hell's fire! If they were to be judged on circumstantial evidence, they were dead as dodo birds already. He rested his chin gently on her soft, tousled hair as he considered what to do next. If she woke up and found herself clinging like a limpet, there would be no living with her; it had been hard enough to talk her into the platonic coexistence of a sleeping bag last night. Diana stirred restlessly in her sleep and his arm tightened around her inadvertently, then relaxed again. This was no time for that!

The best thing to do was evacuate the premises immediately. He set about extricating himself as gently as possible, holding his breath when she moaned softly after he pulled his shoulder away from her head. For a tall man, he moved lithely and succeeded in getting out of their tight quarters before she opened her eyes. She did settle more comfortably into the warmed jacket he had been using for a pillow but he merely grinned at that and left it for her.

Pulling on his boots, he stood and stretched wearily, feeling his back muscles protest fleetingly in the process. He looked again at the sleeping girl and felt a sharp twinge of longing; it would be nice to crawl back in and to the devil with the conventions! He hesitated for just a moment more, frankly enjoying the sight of Diana's softly flushed cheeks and inviting lips. Then he shrugged ruefully and moved quietly across the cabin to the door, where he raised a hand and pounded emphatically on the door panel.

"Come on, Miss Burke, rise and shine. We'd better get stirring if you want a cup of coffee as badly as I do."

Diana heard his voice dimly and tried to tune it out.

"Up, up, up . . . madam," came his unfeeling command again. "The next summons will be a cupful of ice-cold creek water poured on you."

She did open her eyes at that threat. "Did anyone ever tell you that you were a sadistic so-and-so?" she murmured indistinctly.

"Many times. Are you awake now?"

"Yes, I'm awake now," she mimicked defensively. "It's like trying to sleep through an artillery barrage."

"Unpleasant before breakfast, too," he said conversationally. "Now you can see why I've remained a bachelor all these years. I'm going down to the stream . . . if you're not up and about when I get back, I'll use drastic measures."

He was gone before she could focus her attention on him to see if he really meant it. Then, raising her arms, she stretched luxuriously. And winced, just as Matt had winced when muscles protested from their enforced proximity to the floor boards. It was then that she became fully conscious of her location in the sleeping bag and of the jacket pillowing her head.

She shot upright as if a sharp stick had goaded her. Good heavens, what had happened from the time she had started so circumspectly on "her side" of the bag? Her cheeks reddened as she scrambled out of the bed and reached for her shoes. Matthew hadn't said anything, she was thinking as she tried to tie stubborn laces which seemed swollen and stiff to her clumsy fingers. Surely she couldn't have . . .? She perched yoga-fashion on the hard floor, thinking hard and looking like a singularly attractive deity. Then she shrugged her shoulders and got to her feet more stiffly than usual. Matt Reynolds was a gentleman, an explicitly uninterested gentleman, and she was letting her imagination run away with her as she was prone to do.

She brushed down her wrinkled sweater and slacks ineffectually. Her appearance at the moment would cool the ardor of a determined Casanova let alone a glacial scientist who routed her out of bed like some grimy specimen.

Diana ran her fingers through her hair and wished for the umteenth time that she'd had the foresight to tuck a pocket comb in her slacks.

Matt arrived back, throwing the cabin door

wide open. Although his chin could do with a shave, she noted crisply combed hair with water still dripping from it and ruddy cheeks aglow from the icy stream.

"Good thing you're up," he said briskly. "We'd better be on our way. Would you like the sandwich to tide you over until there's a proper breakfast?"

Diana, whose usual morning snack was toast and coffee, shuddered visibly. "No, thank you." She watched him as he set about rolling up the sleeping bag. "You certainly seem in good spirits," she said finally.

"Aren't you?"

"I feel that if I move more than six inches in any direction, I'll shatter into pieces."

He grinned unfeelingly. "That's why I was wishing we had an air mattress. Your reactions to sleeping out sound just like Jill's."

"Your sister?"

He nodded, "She's definitely not the outdoor type. No matter what the season, she used to freeze to death and keep everybody awake complaining bitterly about the cold. If she didn't have an air mattress, she swore she had the Rock of Gibralter smack under the middle of her back. If she did have an air mattress, it was always the one that leaked and morning found her writhing on the ground." He sat back on his haunches and grinned in memory. "It was a great day when she finally got the idea of taking a hot water bottle along; she's even unearthed some strange sleeping garment that has the feet sewn in . . . like they use for babies. The camping trips are certainly a lot more peaceful even if she looks at bit peculiar at bedtime."

Diana felt strangely comforted. "Then I'm not the only one who's complained about being cold?"

"Did you complain?" His smile was wicked. "I don't remember." He enjoyed her obvious moment of discomfiture, then reassured her. "No, of course not. I recall going on a camping trip with a friend of mine when it was so cold that he slept with his glasses on. He felt that anything extra he could wear might help."

An unwilling smile crossed her face. "I have a sneaking suspicion you're just trying to make a greenhorn feel better. If you really want to raise my morale, would you lend me your comb?"

He fished it out solemnly. "Be my guest. Now, get down to the stream; the temperature of that water makes it a shock treatment. I should be about ready to leave when you get back.

She sketched him a mock salute. "When Big Chief Reynolds says go . . . I go."

He took her mockery calmly. "That's good. Because if you didn't, Big Chief Reynolds would be apt to take a piece of firewood to you. If we had one, that is. Now . . . beat it! I'm hungry even if you're not."

By the time Diana had performed her morning ablutions and climbed back up the steep bank, her disposition had improved a thousandfold.

Dawn breaking atop the mountain peaks was a sight unrivaled in her memory and the swift-running stream had effectively washed away the last vestiges of sleep. She had attempted a sketchy toothbrushing with her fingertip and then used Matt's comb to get rid of the tangles in her hair. The wrinkles in her clothes were incorrigible, but evidently wrinkles and camping hazards were old hat to the owner of Killara. Probably he hadn't paid any more attention to them than she had to the mussed condition of his clothing.

She found Matt in the corral cinching the saddle on his satiny horse, who swung his head at her approach and whinnied softly.

"You *are* a beauty," she crooned, advancing slowly and stroking his soft muzzle.

"Now, don't spoil him," Matt told her mildly. "I'm not about to have a splendid animal's training upset by a designing female."

"Puns at this hour of the morning!" She wrinkled her nose disdainfully. "I promise I won't tell your horse how handsome he is ... even though Jim Dodge did call him 'a magnificent palomino.'"

"I don't know what Jim said," he replied, "but he's a sure-enough palomino and one of the finest trail horses in this part of the country. You can steal the silver at Killara and it

81

wouldn't raise my blood pressure, but make off with my horse and I'll have the vigilantes after you."

"I'll remember," she said solemnly. "Now you're beginning to sound like the Western movies I saw when I was a child."

"I'm feeling ancient this morning but I didn't know it was as bad as that."

"Stop fishing for compliments, Dr. Reynolds." She watched him strap the blanket roll behind the saddle. "What does trail horse mean?"

"It's the designation of a working Western horse as opposed to a horse ridden merely for pleasure," he said briskly. "Trail horses have to allow their riders to open gates without dismounting, go up next to objects flapping in the wind without spooking, sidle along fallen fence railing, or back up at an unspoken command. Bob here," he gave the intelligent-looking animal a proud slap on the rump, "brought home a blue ribbon from the international show last year. Jill was riding him. She's tried everything but blackmail to get him away from me ever since."

"Do you still show him?"

"Lord no, I don't have the time anymore." He gave the saddle girth a final test. "That should do it. If you'll wait here, I'll give a final once-over to the cabin and then we'll be on our way."

She watched him stride off and gazed again in admiration at the beautiful palomino beside her. He was untethered except for the braided reins which were dropped casually on the ground, but he stood quietly, cropping casually on a clump of grass by her foot.

"Carmen could take lessons from you," Diana murmured to him softly, "and maybe I could too." She turned and sauntered over to lean on the corral gate and wait for Matt's return.

He wasn't long in coming. "All set?"

"Yes, I'm ready. This corral must be a busy place," she said, more to make conversation than anything else. "Even Carmen seems to have left her mark."

Matt gave her a sharp look. "What do you know about Carmen?"

"Actually, just enough to get out of her way quickly." She switched to the defensive. "Why? What have I done wrong now?"

"Stop flaring up," he gave her shoulder an absent squeeze. "I was surprised that you recognized her hoofprint. You're a better spotter than I gave you credit for."

"At gathering unimportant information and trivia, I'm unsurpassed," she said airily. "It's on the important stuff that I'm apt to be absent-minded."

He pulled the reins over Bob's head. "Well, pay attention to what you're doing and get aboard. I'll give you a leg up."

"Don't be too vigorous," she said, approaching him warily. "I'm sure Bob is too polite to

83

give me a horse laugh if I land on the other side but I'll bet you aren't." Fortunately, she was able to remain on top, albeit with an ungraceful lurch. She gripped the pommel tightly. "Now what?"

For an answer, he merely stepped into the stirrup as easily as she would swing aboard a bus and came up into the saddle behind her.

"Inhale a little," he commanded.

She tried to draw herself forward and out of his way as much as possible.

"Relax," he said, amusement in his tone. "You don't have to clutch the saddle horn; I won't let you fall."

His strong arms encased her firmly and she let her body ease back against his broad chest. Bob moved in a graceful circle near the corral at an unspoken command.

"Are we looking for something or someone?" Diana's tone was uneasy.

"Certainly not someone. Your 'friend' made tracks long ago." Matt exerted a slight pressure on the reins and Bob headed toward a broad trail leading away from the stream. "We'd better be on our way, too; there's a lot to do today."

"This isn't the trail I followed."

"I know." He shifted slightly in the saddle to allow her to fit even more comfortably against him. "Is that better?"

She nodded. "Fine, thanks. Where does this trail lead?"

"It's the main trail from Killara to the cabin. There's a more rugged one from the cabin on up to the summit."

"I presume it's shorter than the creek trail."

"You presume right." He sounded absent-minded. "Belt up for a while . . . I want to think."

"Now who's irritable before breakfast," she chided, but without rancor and let her head rest against the broad shoulder behind her as if it were the most natural thing in the world.

They rode down the wide trail, now dappled with thin morning sun, in quiet contentment, the only sounds the clop of Bob's hooves, an occasional rustle from a startled chipmunk, or the shriek of a Canada jay overhead.

The time passed quickly and distance capsuled under Bob's even strides.

"Isn't this too much weight for him?" Diana felt compelled to ask at one point.

"Certainly not." Matt's arm tightened around her. "If it were, I'd make you walk. Are you enjoying it?"

"Anyone who didn't would be stark, raving bonkers." Her voice remained casual only with an effort. "Was that Killara I saw through that last break in the trees?"

"Uh-huh. We circle down at this point. With luck, we should get in before the household's up."

"I meant to ask you before," her tone was preoccupied, "what does Killara mean? I suppose it's Indian . . ." 85

"No. Actually it's an Australian aboriginal word meaning 'Always there.' A friend of my father's from Sydney named it years ago."

"Always there ..." her voice explored the meaning softly. "That's just right, isn't it?"

There was a pause before he answered. "So you feel that way too." His hands tightened visibly on the reins. "I should have known better than to underestimate Aunt Violet."

"What do you mean by that?"

"Nothing that's worth discussing at this hour."

Bob came out onto the dirt path leading to the Killara stable and quickened his pace.

"There are cars all over the place," Diana said, still confused by Matt's stilted tone and her reaction to it. "What in the world is going on?"

"Oh, help ..." His groan was heartfelt. "They're all here."

"Who's here?"

"Mrs. Lee, the cook ... who's a nice old lady with a wagging tongue long enough to cover the entire county with gossip, and her niece who doesn't know one end of a dust rag from the other."

"I don't see ..."

"And," he interrupted ruthlessly, "my sister Jill who never misses a thing. I only hope to heaven that she's used her head this time."

"... what all the fuss is about," Diana finished determinedly.

"You Easterners may take it a little more

lightly," he said, "but in this part of the country, six-thirty in the morning is hardly the time for the hero to bring the girl home after a night out."

"Surely they won't think . . ." her voice trailed off dismally.

"No? Wouldn't you?" He didn't wait for her to reply. "It doesn't matter. We'll tell them the truth and let Mrs. Lee do her best with it. I was just hoping to keep your reputation unscathed." He directed Bob toward the front drive as he spoke.

Just then the side door banged open and a beautiful blond girl whose hair was wound in a graceful braid coronet came hurrying out to meet them.

"Good morning," she said pleasantly, "how did your morning ride go?"

Matt pulled Bob to a stop and looked down at her without expression. "Very well, thanks. Diana, this is my sister Jill Reynolds. Jill . . . Diana Burke . . . a legacy of Aunt Violet."

Diana felt a high-powered glance go over her from a pair of deep blue eyes.

"So you're the birthday present," Jill drawled, not unkindly. "You'd better come in and have some breakfast." She glanced up at her brother. "I told Madame Lee that you were out for an early morning ride with an old friend of the family. It's a darned good thing for you two that I arrived a half hour before the household staff."

Matt's sigh of relief was evident. "Thank God you used your head."

Jill's glance at him was thoughtful. "And thank the Lord yours came through unscathed. Mrs. Lee has had me on the verge of the screaming meemies since her news this morning."

"What's uppermost on her mind today?" Matt dismounted and reached up to help Diana as she slid down beside him.

"Something definitely more exciting than her usual fare." Jill matched her brother's calm. "One of the men down at the junction discovered a body by the Killara turn-off this morning when he was putting out his milk cans for pickup."

"A dead man!" Matt glanced sharply at her. "Anyone we knew?"

"Not according to Mrs. Lee. The authorities believe he was a Canadian citizen. He'd been terribly beaten and left to die. Anyhow, when I heard about people lying around dead and then discovered your beds weren't slept in . . ."

He cut her off with a gesture. "What's next on the docket?"

"You mean with the authorities?" his sister asked. "Well, anybody who has seen or heard anything pertinent in the way of evidence must get in touch. Otherwise, all the Killara residents are in the clear." She shot a quick look at Diana's pale face. "I'm sure that you could use some breakfast at this point. Just give me a few minutes to get Mrs. Lee organized." A quick smile and then she hurried back up the path to the house.

Diana's knees suddenly lost their starch as she leaned against Bob's smooth flank. She turned slowly toward Matt who was standing immobile, frowning down at the dirt path. "I think," she said, "that I'm too tired to live up to your way of life around here."

"I know damned well that I am," he ground out through clenched teeth. "Has it occurred to you that the dead man or his murderer might well have been the one who kept you in the cabin?"

"There was a niggling suspicion."

"And that you're lucky not to have ended up with your neck in a sling, as well?"

"If you keep up with the cheerful talk, you're going to spoil my breakfast for sure."

His mouth thinned to a straight line as he swallowed an impolite remark, then turned abruptly to swing up in the saddle. "I would like to know what the hell is going on around here," was his terse comment before he rode off, leaving a cloud of dust to settle around her.

Diana stared after him stoically. That last remark wasn't like Matt Reynolds, she was sure. It wasn't like him at all. For the first time, Killara loomed as a possible threat to her physical safety. She had suspected all the way down from the cabin that Killara's master had already become a threat to her peace of mind.

Chapter Four

When Matt reappeared, it was at the splendidly carved oak refectory table some forty-five minutes later.

"I was wondering when you were coming for breakfast," Jill said from her place at the end of it. "Are you going to settle down long enough to eat something?"

"Certainly I am." Matt was very much the urbane older brother in pressed slacks and immaculate sports jacket. "I'm sorry to have been so long but I had to take care of Bob and change clothes." He gave a casual glance at their plates. "It's a good thing you and Miss Burke didn't wait for me."

The swinging door to the kitchen that had prompted Diana's perverse temper two nights before opened in response to Jill's buzzer and a girl in her late teens bounced through.

"Good morning, Dr. Reynolds." Her voice was full of youthful ebullience. "Want eggs and bacon, as usual?"

Matt winced slightly at her loud tone, but his reply was beyond reproach. "Yes, thanks,

Mavis. It's nice to have you back. Did you have a good time on your vacation?"

The girl brushed her long, straight hair behind her ears and gave him a wide smile. "Fab ... Dr. Reynolds ... simply fab! It would have been more fun coming back, though, if you hadn't sent Harvey up to the high range."

"He'll be back before you know it."

"That's what you think." Her giggle was infectious. "I'll bring your eggs right away." The door swung shut behind her.

"Harvey is one of the men," Jill translated for Diana, "and the only reason we can keep someone Mavis's age this far from the bright lights."

"Not the only reason," Matt contradicted. "Her aunt does her part by keeping a heavy thumb on her social schedule." He took a sip of coffee. "How Mavis can see through that hair amazes me. I've seen more attractive fringes on sheepdogs."

"Go back to your grapefruit." Jill's expression was amused. "Long hair is all the rage, so don't be so stodgy. At least, I was able to pry her transistor radio away from her." She turned to Diana. "I thought I'd better before Matt got violent on the subject."

Conversation stopped abruptly as the swinging door was propelled open again by Mavis bearing a plateful of scrambled eggs and bacon. "Here you go, Dr. Reynolds. Would you like anything else?"

"No thanks." He gave her an absent-minded

91

smile which caused a pleased flush on the girl's cheeks.

She straightened her apron awkwardly. "Just buzz if you do," she managed finally, and escaped through the door again.

"It's a good thing you're leaving," Jill said ironically. "With Mavis and the opposite sex, propinquity seems to be the only requisite. By the time you get back, Harvey should be down for a weekend and her love life can resolve itself."

Matt merely snorted and picked up a piece of toast.

Diana cleared her throat. "I didn't know you were leaving, Dr. Reynolds."

He concentrated on his breakfast determinedly. "I didn't have a good chance to tell you, Miss Burke. Actually, I just found out for sure yesterday morning when I checked in with the lab. The man who was supposed to read a paper at a meeting in London has come down with a nasty virus and I've been asked to take his place."

"London!" Belatedly, she tried to recover her composure. "How long do you plan to be gone?"

"Only a week at the most." He pulled his glasses from his shirt pocket, put them on, and gave her one of his level glances. "I have enough work started so that you can get on with the typing I mentioned before. Jill will be here to keep you company."

"At least some of the time." His sister pushed back a strand of the pale, blond hair that was caught up atop her head, giving her a piquant old-fashioned look. "Don't forget, I'm due up in Vancouver for Sheelah's wedding later in the week. You're supposed to be there too."

"I'd forgotten that." He frowned. "At least Mrs. Lee and Mavis will be around here."

"I'm sure I'll get along just fine." Diana recovered her dignity with an effort after the shock of his announcement. If the man chose to treat her as an unwanted house guest after their night in the cabin, she could show the same lack of interest.

But was there really any change? There had been nothing in his remarks or overnight behavior to indicate he had the slightest interest in her personally other than to see that she was safely cared for.

Why then did she suddenly feel as if she had been left completely bereft? It should be pleasant to spend some days in peace and quiet at Killara; there would be no listening consciously for familiar footsteps. No waiting, as she had waited at the breakfast table for him to make a belated appearance. No listening, no waiting ... no nothing.

"How you got Miss Burke to turn from interior decorating to typing, I'll never understand," Jill was saying, her eyes bright with mischief. "Did he threaten you, Miss Burke?"

"Diana ... please ... Miss Burke is too formal. No, he didn't threaten me."

"I simply told her I didn't want the house changed," Matt interrupted tersely, crumpling his napkin on the table and standing up. "I want to see the sheriff for a little while. Jill, could you do my packing for me? You know what I need. I'll get Jake to drive me to the airport afterwards and then he can bring the car back here and stick around in the bunkhouse while I'm gone. He's been dying of boredom ever since we pensioned him off so it will be good for him to have something to do."

Jill looked puzzled but said calmly, "All right if you want to, but I don't see why we need him."

"If nothing else, he can take care of the horses. They're eating their heads off and just getting fat without any exercise. I should be back in an hour or so but I'll have to leave in a hurry then, so have my bag ready."

Jill stared after his disappearing figure with amusement. "And that's that!" She turned to Diana and grinned. "Did you ever hear more brotherly commands? Talk about autocrats at the breakfast table! He's not like himself at all this morning. I can't decide whether you've had a bad effect on him or whether it was hearing about that dead man near the junction."

"I'm sure I didn't have any kind of effect on Dr. Reynolds," Diana said definitely, pushing back her chair. "That was a marvelous breakfast. Your Mrs. Lee may not have the sweetest disposition in the world, but she can certainly cook."

"Then you noticed the appraisal you were getting when I introduced you earlier?"

Diana laughed ruefully. "I'm sure she'll have plenty of questions if she ever finds herself alone with me."

Jill stood up and motioned for Diana to precede her out to the stairway. "Then if I were you, I'd take great care to avoid that situation. Mrs. Lee's interrogation techniques would make the sheriff's look tame."

"Do you honestly think your brother is upset about this murder happening so close to Killara?"

"Could be, although the victim was a stranger, so I can't see why Matt need be concerned." Jill paused at the top of the stairs. "Of course it's terrible when you can't escape city-type crimes in a place like this. Killara used to be a refuge for all of us but these days there's no longer a place to get away from it all." She shrugged and made a wry face. "Come on in and talk to me while I pack Matt's things. I know the drill so well by now that it's a cinch."

"I'll be glad to if you're sure I won't make you forget something vital."

"Not a chance." Jill led the way into a spacious bedroom that was almost austere in its decoration. A single bed was covered with a striped Indian design bedspread in shades of brown and green. The same colors were repeated at the long windows. Grasscloth of a neutral shade was on the walls and provided a background for a series of Winslow Homer prints. Two deep chairs in brown were separated by a lamp table piled high with books.

Diana sank into one of the chairs. "This is very nice. I can see why your brother doesn't want any of the decorating changed."

"What a dandy thing to say!" Jill's face flushed with pleasure.

"Did you do it?" Diana's interest was genuine.

"Sort of . . . in bits and pieces."

"Then why did your aunt bother to send me all this way?"

"Oh, Aunt Vi . . ." Jill threw a smile at her as she took a brown leather suitcase from the closet and spread it open on the bed. "There's no accounting for her whims. One year she sent Matt an entire truckload of guinea hens because she heard their eggs were good for you. Those hens made the most unholy racket; I thought we'd never get rid of them."

"What finally happened?"

"Matt persuaded one of the chicken ranchers down in the valley to take them off his hands. Another time we got a wire from an air freight company alerting us to receive some highland cattle from Scotland that Aunt Vi had decided we needed. You know the ones . . . with horns like Brahmas and straggly long coats of hair.

Thank heavens we stopped that shipment before it left the British Isles."

"Unfortunately, no one was around to stop me," Diana said meekly.

"You're a little different."

"Not much. No long horns and I don't make as much racket as a guinea hen but your brother probably thinks the other gifts were easier to get rid of."

Jill looked up from her careful packing of a black dinner jacket. "It's hard to find out what Matt thinks. All I know is that he called me in Oregon yesterday to get back here pronto. He felt out of his depth with an unchaperoned guest and he wasn't looking forward to an indefinite stay in the bunkhouse. Besides, he said it was time I got back to work."

"What did he mean by that?"

"Oh, I do scientific illustrations for the research group down at the lab. I majored in art in college and found that I enjoyed illustrating some of Matt's articles in the scientific journals. After that, one thing just seemed to follow the other. I can work on a part-time basis at some seasons of the year, which lets me follow the horse shows or do some traveling. Since Mother and Father died in an automobile collision ten years ago, Matt has been the one who had to watch over me. Now that I've finally got my degree, he can let up on being the heavy parent." She was pulling shoe protectors over a pair of loafers before tucking them in one end

97

of the bag. "He was a wonderful support all the times I needed a helping hand or thought I'd perish with loneliness. Now I wish he wouldn't take life so seriously. It would be nice if he'd go off and sow a few wild oats of his own."

"Maybe he will in London."

Jill wrinkled her nose derisively. "It's easy to see you haven't been to one of the august scientific gatherings. Their idea of a riotous time is to look at somebody's slides of seal rookeries. At the cocktail parties before the banquets, it's the old story of divided sexes—husbands on one side of the room discussing Smythe-Thomas's chance for promotion, while across the way their long-suffering wives count the stripes on the wallpaper."

"You make it sound awful."

Jill giggled. "I'm exaggerating really. I've neglected to mention some of the handsome creatures who take part in those doings. Matt gets mad if I whisk them off to go dancing instead of letting them participate in his panel discussions. Isn't that just like an older brother!"

"I'm afraid I wouldn't know," Diana smiled sympathetically at her. "I was the only one in the nest."

"Did you always want to be an interior decorator?"

"Nearly always. I was lucky to find a place with David Royle's firm. That's how I met your aunt . . . when our company did her penthouse."

"I know." Jill added a small pile of handkerchiefs to the neatly packed suitcase. "Aunt Vi calls us fairly frequently, although she hasn't been out to see us for a year or two. That's probably the reason she didn't know I'd been working on the house."

"And doing a beautiful job of it," Diana added firmly. "If you wanted to work in the East, I'm sure David could use you."

"No thanks." Jill put her hands on her hips and straightened like a lazy cat. "I can't imagine leaving this part of the country for very long." She grinned. "Whoever finally takes me has to take my horses, as well." Giving a calculating look at the open bag she said, "I think that finishes the packing. Matt can look it over when he changes and see if I've forgotten anything. Now I'd better go down and discuss menus with Mrs. Lee so we'll be sure of having something to eat. Want to come along?"

"No thanks. I'll check the typing that your brother mentioned so I'll know for sure just what he wants me to do. Then I think I'll walk down to the pasture and admire your horses."

"They'll love the company if Carmen will let them get near you." Jill held the door open for her to pass through. "Stop in the kitchen and pick up a few carrots. I always keep a crisperful just for that."

Diana gave her a wry smile. "From what Jim

Dodge told me, they had better be long carrots if I'm to have any fingers left."

"Jim and Carmen don't hit it off . . . that's for sure. He would have gotten rid of her long ago if Matt hadn't been so stubborn."

"I'm glad Dr. Reynolds held firm. At least your foreman provides some local color—he looks and sounds exactly like the men in those Western commercials." She hesitated and then went on to say, "I also got the feeling that he knew it."

Jill paused by the dining room archway. "Kim's a pet, but a little like a dose of medicine. You know . . . 'to be taken with care, and if symptoms persist, discontinue use immediately.'"

Diana was still thinking of her remark with amusement some time later as she made her way down to Carmen's pasture. Jill's naïveté extended only so far, evidently, and she had fixed Jim Dodge's character with deadly precision. All the same, the physical makeup of the man alone, to say nothing of his splendid drawl, would certainly make him an asset at any social gathering.

A rude, horsey snort interrupted her reflections as she approached the fence and found Carmen there to meet her. The burro's rough coat had not been improved by what was evidently a recent roll in the dust.

"You look like something that somebody threw away," Diana told her frankly. "I can't imagine how those two beauties," she nodded toward the glossy Dee and Dum who were watching from a safe distance, "even allow you in the pasture with them."

Carmen snorted again and edged closer to the fence.

"You're limping," Diana said in sudden concern. "What's the matter, you poor baby?"

"Carmen's been called lots of things . . ." Matt's voice sounded behind her, "but 'poor baby' is a new one."

Diana turned, confused. "I didn't hear you coming. Carmen snuffles like a noisy steam engine." She noted his subdued charcoal suit worn with a pale blue shirt and matching tie. The inevitable glasses were tucked carelessly in his breast pocket. "I should think they'd fall out," she said absently.

He must have been reading her mind because he poked at the frames casually. "They do, every once in a while. I always have a second pair along."

"Are they for reading?" The query was out before she was conscious of it.

He seemed amused. "And seeing. I came down to say good-bye."

"Oh." Her tone was deflated. "Jill said you were cutting it fine . . . the polar flight to London, isn't it?"

He nodded.

"Well, have a good trip and a pleasant time. London's a marvelous place so don't work too hard." She tried desperately to think of something other than the usual clichés. "I looked over your copy in the library . . . the notes seem clear enough."

"If you have any trouble with the spelling, just ask Jill. She's familiar with most of the terms." He frowned suddenly. "I've told her and now I'm telling you to stay close by the house until the sheriff gets this trouble solved."

"I'd almost forgotten about that," she confessed. "Is there anything new?"

"They've sent the fingerprints along for identification." He shoved his hands into his trouser pockets and stared glumly at Carmen. "From the way the man was dressed, it looked as if he might have come from abroad fairly recently. There was a Rome label in his tie and the shoes he was wearing were of European make."

"That doesn't sound like the usual criminal type."

"Not around here, at any rate," he conceded. "More like the kind you read about in the Eastern tabloids."

"Did you have to try to identify him?"

He nodded, his lips tightening to a thin line. "The sheriff asked me to. The body was in pretty bad shape."

She uttered a soft sound of sympathy.

"It's a pity anyone has to die like that," he continued evenly, "without the slightest semblance of dignity."

"Remember your 'Thanatopsis'?" she prompted. "'Approach thy grave like one who wraps the drapery of his couch about him and lies down to pleasant dreams.' "

He nodded. "I remember. Well," he reached out to scratch Carmen's muzzle, "from what I could see in this case, there were no pleasant dreams . . . it was strictly the nightmare variety." He shifted restlessly against the fence. "Be careful down here with Carmen. She's a good old girl but she has definite likes and dislikes."

"Jim Dodge warned me. Did you notice that she's limping?"

"Is she? I'd better take a look." He caught hold of the burro's rope bridle and led her along the fence.

"Look out or you'll get gray hair all over your suit."

"It wouldn't be the first time," he said absently. "She's favoring her left foreleg. I don't think it's serious, but I'll tell Jake to look after it as soon as he delivers me to the airport." He brushed casually at his sleeve where it had rubbed against Carmen's dusty nose.

"Let me." Diana brushed forcefully at the material and picked off the stubborn burro hairs. "You looked so elegant when you came down here. Heavens, you can't go to London all mussed."

She missed the slow smile he directed at the top of her head. "I'll be plenty mussed after ten hours' sitting in the plane." He glanced at his watch. "Lord, I have to get going or I'll never make it."

Diana stepped back in some confusion. What did one do now ... shake hands or ...?

He was looking down at her just as uncertainly. "Take care of yourself," he said finally. "You know, I really came down to apologize for losing my temper with you earlier."

"Forget it," she said indistinctly. "We were both upset."

Carmen chose that moment to poke an inquisitive nose toward Diana's jacket pocket where two fresh carrots reposed. Her sudden motion startled Diana and she stumbled against Matt's chest. His arms shot out protectively to keep her from falling. She looked up apologetically just as his lips descended to cover hers. It was a hurried kiss, but remarkably thorough nonetheless.

"Matt ... are you coming?" Jill's voice called from the drive and an automobile horn honked twice peremptorily.

Matt raised his head and put Diana gently from him. Her cheeks were flushed and she stared up at his intent face in confusion. He gave her a long, level look and then turned to give Carmen a farewell pat. "I always knew I kept you around for some reason, old girl," he said roughly. Halfway up the path, he hesitated and turned to call back to the still bemused Diana. "I think that should be worth two carrots, at least ... don't you?" She saw the fleeting remnants of a mocking grin before he disappeared around the corner of the house.

Jill found her still patting the burro when she came down the path a little later. "Well, Matt finally got off," she said in some relief. "I've never known him to leave things so late." She glanced casually over at the dark-haired girl. "Did he give you the last minute instructions he was talking about?"

"Um-hum." Diana's tone was dreamy. "I'm to ask you if I can't figure out the spelling."

"Well, there's no point in working yourself to death," Jill said briskly. "You can copy in the afternoon after we've gone riding in the morning. Dee and Dum could use the exercise." She glanced again at the silent girl beside her. "You do ride, don't you?"

"Hmm? Oh, I'm sorry . . ." Diana brought her thoughts back with an effort. "Ride? Well, in a way. A friend of mine, Carlo Mangini, took me out a few times when I was in northern Italy last year. He was a magnificient horseman and he was appalled to hear that a shetland pony years ago had given me my only experience in riding."

"I should think so," said Jill. "How did your lessons go?"

"Carlo tried . . ." Diana said dubiously. "I can stick on top these days, but not with any finesse."

Jill grinned at her amiably. "Then I'll try to add the finesse."

105

So it went for the next three days, starting with brisk rides around the pasture the first morning and progressing into the valley after that.

"I promised Matt not to get too far into the rough country while he's gone," Jill said as she led the way back on the third day. "I suppose we could borrow Jake to 'ride shotgun,' but I hate to take him away from his work."

"And I'd just as soon not have any onlookers until I get better at staying on the back of Dee," Diana said, patting the glossy bay mare as they pulled up by the stable. She swung off, sighing with relief.

"You're doing better . . . much better," Jill told her judiciously. "Not nearly so much elbow-flapping today."

"I discovered that I'd never get off the ground that way so I changed my tactics," Diana said solemnly as she stretched gingerly. "This afternoon I won't need an entire box of baking soda in my bath . . . just half a box."

Jill laughed and looped her reins casually on the fence. "There's Jake coming," she waved at the approaching figure. "He can do the unsaddling for us today." She took Diana's elbow and steered her purposefully up the path. "I've got to get packed to leave this afternoon for that wedding in Vancouver and I want your advice on a dress. I can't decide whether it's too formal for the spinster dinner." She hesitated as she saw a camper round the front drive and then give a spurt to pull up beside them. "Hi, Jim," she called as he stepped out of the truck. "I thought you'd be back before this."

The big foreman came around the hood, nodding a greeting to Diana as she stood beside Jill. "Howdy, ladies, guess I am a little late." He pulled off his big hat and held it awkwardly in his hands. "I just got up on the range and that old ulcer of mine started playin' up again."

"Oh, Jim, I am sorry." Jill put an anxious hand on his sleeve. "Why didn't you let us know?"

"I didn't have time," he confessed. "The way I was feelin' I knew I'd better get to the doc right away, so I did. Then he chucked me in the hospital for a couple of days until it calmed down."

"How are you feeling now?" Diana asked.

"Lots better," he answered with a grin. "I hear that Matt got off all right."

"How did you know about that?" Jill wanted to know.

"I came in a little earlier and got all the drift from Jake. He told me you two girls were out for a ride." His strong fingers fiddled with the brim of his hat. "He also told me about the trouble with that body they discovered down at the crossroads."

Jill nodded. "There's been lots more excitement than usual. Nothing new on it, though. Jake heard they'd identified the man ... somebody with a long criminal record."

107

"I didn't know about all this," Diana said. "What kind of crimes?"

"Mainly to do with narcotics," Jill reported. "I guess I forgot to mention it."

"What was a man like that doing in this neck of the woods?" Jim wanted to know.

Jill shook her head ruefully. "That's the question everybody's asking and if the sheriff knows anything, he's not putting it out for general consumption."

"Oh well, I suppose we'll learn in time." Jim stirred restlessly. "I wish this stomach of mine hadn't put me so far behind schedule."

"You'll catch up," Jill told him in a soothing tone. "Besides, you'd better take it easy or you'll be right back in the hospital again." Her eyes narrowed as she surveyed him. "You don't look very well right now."

Jim snorted. "Don't you start that. I promised the doc I'd take it easy."

Jill managed a severe look. "See that you do. At least Diana will have you around for company while I'm gone to Vancouver."

His grin dispelled any look of invalidism. "You bet! And if she doesn't need anything special, I might try to dream up something."

Diana adopted Jill's severe tone. "Remember what your doctor said. Besides, if I keep up with these riding lessons, I'll end on an invalid's couch myself. I didn't know that I possessed as many muscles as I do . . . all aching and creaking."

Jim grinned in sympathy. "If you're trying to keep up with Jill . . . it's no wonder."

"You're both a couple of lilies," the blond girl scoffed as she took Diana's elbow and urged her toward the house. "I've got to pack. Take care of yourself while I'm gone, Jim."

He replaced his hat and climbed back in the driver's seat. "I'll do that. Don't go falling for any of those Canadians, y'hear?"

"I won't," Jill promised, and Diana gave him a brief wave of farewell before the foreman spurted off toward his cottage.

Mavis intercepted them as they stepped into the front hall. "I'm glad you've come, Miss Jill. Dr. Reynolds is calling from London."

"Hurry, Jill," Diana pushed her toward the study. "I'll be up in my room if you want me." She watched Jill's slim figure disappear through the study door and then walked slowly up to her room. She sank thoughtfully in a chair by the window. Her legs, now trimly attired in beige Western riding pants, stretched out in front of her.

What could Matt want that required a call from Britain? She thought again of his last day at Killara and frowned slightly. His rapid change of mood had caught her unawares, and she had responded more freely to that sudden kiss than she had intended. Darn the man! In his way, he was just as irritating and sure of himself as Jim Dodge. Both of them had obviously had their way with the feminine sex for far too long. It was time for her to change the ground rules. Dr. Reynolds might think he was enjoying a bit of fluff close to home, but next time he'd have to find another partner. The buzzer sounded on her phone and she got up to answer it.

"Did you want me, Jill?"

"No . . . I do." Even across the miles of ocean, his amused voice made her knees suddenly go weak. "I need to ask a favor, Miss Burke."

She sat down abruptly on the edge of the bed. "Of course, Dr. Reynolds."

"First of all, do you have your passport with you?"

"Yes," her voice was puzzled. "I thought I might need it for identification if I went up to Canada."

"Good!" His relief was evident. "That will save time. I need a box of special photographic slides over here. Jill will assemble them for you. With any luck, you can still get on this afternoon's flight. I probably won't be able to meet you at Heathrow because of our meeting schedule, but the conference is at the Victoria on Park Lane, so just take a taxi and check in there. I'll put the reservation under your name. Don't bother with a typewriter . . . I'll arrange to get one here. Any questions?" He was brisk and as calm as if arranging for a trip to the corner drugstore.

She sat as if stunned.

"Miss Burke? Diana . . ." his tone was suddenly concerned. "Are you all right? Can you come?"

An idiotic smile spread slowly over her face and its warmth penetrated all the way to her toes. So much for propinquity and changes in ground rules. "Yes . . . I'm here." She finally managed to get the words out. "And thank you, Dr. Reynolds . . . Matt . . . I'd love to come."

Chapter Five

As usual, London was massive, slightly moldy and damp, but altogether marvelous. Diana took a deep breath as she came out of the Kensington air terminal and smiled in utter delight. Tokyo might be bigger, New York more bustling, but for sheer, unadulterated charm, London was the winner-take-all.

She glanced up at the gray morning sky; at least the rain was holding off for the time being. The taxi queue was short and she was soon on her way down past the green of Hyde Park.

Already the streets were thronged with traffic and pedestrians were emerging from the underground stations but in a considerably more leisurely way than their American counterparts. At discreet intervals, signs advertising morning coffees and afternoon teas were seen along the busy, tree-lined street. The taxi passed an efficient-looking nursemaid wheeling her charge along the sidewalk in an enormous British pram. Behind her were two tiny shops, one bearing a fish monger's sign and the other with the lettering of a timber merchant. A tall young man wearing a bowler and carrying the inevitable furled umbrella was unlocking the door of a corner shop. In New York, all of those things would have attracted stares; in London, they were accepted as an integral part of the background.

The taxi rounded Hyde Park Corner and she caught a glimpse of pageantry in the distance as the royal Horse Guards headed down the bridle path toward the palace. Then suddenly she was at the hotel and had to dive for her change purse and hastily start multiplying. Nine shillings, tuppence plus the tip . . . she scrabbled in the coins and evidently arrived at a satisfactory amount, for the driver said "Ta, Miss" in a pleasant tone of voice. Her two suitcases disappeared with the assistance of the doorman and the porter while she followed meekly up the stairs to the reception desk.

"Miss Burke?" The young man behind the registration card was attired in a black coat and striped gray morning trousers. "Will you register, please. Dr. Reynolds specified that you would like a view of the park and Hyde Park Corner. Would the fifteenth floor be satisfactory?"

"It sounds very nice. May I go right up?"

"Certainly." He handed the key to a formally dressed counterpart who suddenly appeared beside her. "Mr. Gibson will take you up."

113

"Thank you." She swung back to the desk abruptly. "Were there any messages for me?"

"No, Miss Burke," the clerk's tone was as impeccable as his white collar. "Nothing."

"All right . . . thank you." She turned to follow the other hotel man to the elevator. He was pale, effete, and looked like a window display figure with his carefully controlled expression. Diana felt as if she should ask if he needed help in carrying the key and then shook herself mentally and blamed it all on jet fatigue. He led her carefully down the hall to her room and unlocked the door.

The room was lovely, with a magnificent view over the park and high enough to change the noise of the traffic into a discreet hum rather than an annoying roar. Her guide gave her an elementary lesson in turning on and off the television set, as if the principles of the BBC might be beyond her transatlantic mind, and then offered a similar course on air conditioning with the thermostat dial. Finally, he bowed in farewell, and she caught herself just in time to keep from bowing ceremoniously in return as the door closed behind him.

At the sound of the discreet slam, she immediately pulled off her shoes and sank back on the queen-sized bed. Then she yawned mightily; if only the passengers of polar flights could swallow a time capsule along with their dinner so that they would feel as if they were on London time rather than being achingly aware that

114

their stomachs and minds were still slogging along in the Pacific Daylight zone. She yawned again, felt a moment's guilt that she was lying in her dacron knit suit rather than something more suitable for lounging, and then surrendered by closing her eyes.

She didn't open them again until there was a disturbance at the door, an insistent knocking that sounded as if it had been going on for some time.

"Just a minute," she called, stumbling to her feet and looking at her watch simultaneously. Almost two o'clock! She had been asleep for over three hours. The knocking continued, and she gave up the half-hearted attempt to find her shoes and hurried to open the door.

"I was getting worried about you," Matt greeted her simply.

Diana was only capable of staring happily at him in return. As she searched for something appropriate to say, his warm smile faded suddenly.

"Are you all right?" he asked in some concern.

She swallowed, suddenly appallingly aware of how she must look with a face flushed from sleep, hair in disarray, and a wrinkled suit despite the manufacturer's claims to the contrary.

"I'm fine," she stammered finally, wishing she had stopped to find her shoes, as he literally seemed to tower over her. "Just fine . . . I was

115

asleep," she pushed her hair back with a fretful gesture, "and I can't find my shoes."

"If I could come in," he said with some amusement, "I could help you hunt for them."

"Oh heavens, of course." She stepped back and closed the door behind him.

"Are these the ones you were looking for?" He held up the green pumps that were half-hidden under the end of the bedspread.

"Yes, thanks." She took them from him in relief and slipped them on. "Sit down, won't you." She gestured toward the pair of chintz covered chairs in front of the big window. "Let me comb my hair and try to look a little more civilized."

"Stop fussing . . . you look fine," he said easily, but she had disappeared into the bathroom, leaving the door ajar behind her. "Did you have a good flight?"

"Yes, thanks . . . very uneventful. The only excitement was when we stopped at Winnipeg to refuel and they forgot to put the final reel of the movie aboard." She poked her head around the door momentarily to give him an impish grin. "A pity because it was a John Wayne film and I think he's terrific."

"I'll remember that." He surveyed her carefully as she came back into the room, still looking flustered but with shiny chestnut hair neatly in place and a fresh application of lipstick. "You look very nice, but you'd better take it easy this afternoon."

She made a gesture of protest. "A nap was all I needed. Your box of slides is right here." She moved over to get a thin leather case from the top of the television and hand it to him.

"Slides?" His voice was puzzled and then his perplexed look faded. "Oh yes, of course. I'll take them with me. Thanks very much for bringing them."

"They really brought me, didn't they?" She sank into the chair across from him. "I feel like a very expensive messenger at this point, so you'd better put me to work."

"There's not much to do . . . just some notes typed later on if you could manage."

"Easily." She was amused at his diffident manner. "Surely there must be something else . . ."

"We'll see. Jill said that everything was going along all right at home."

She nodded. "Smooth as silk. She was crushed that she couldn't come, but she was involved as a bridesmaid and practically en route to Vancouver when you called."

"Mmm, that's what she said." His mouth twitched ever so slightly in amusement. "How's Carmen getting along?"

Despite her best intentions, Diana could feel the heat suffusing her cheekbones. "Jake says she's almost back to normal," she murmured with her glance determinedly on the carpet. "He felt the limp came from a pulled muscle."

"She's eating well?"

"Heavens yes! She certainly consumes carrots with enthusiasm. Why yesterday, she ate one out of my fingers as daintily . . ." her voice trailed off as she noted his mocking grin. "I'm sure you heard all this from Jill, and I have no right to keep you from your work." Her tone was stiff with embarrassment.

He shot a rueful glance at his watch. "It's not all that late, Miss Burke. Or since we're two foreigners in a strange land . . . how about making it Diana? I shouldn't tease you, but it is a temptation."

"To watch me squirm like a pinned fly," she told him severely. "Jill should have warned me."

"So she should." He settled more comfortably in his chair and stretched long legs out in front of him. "I meant to ask about the latest news on the mystery man."

She crossed her knees and then, as her short skirt hiked up, decided to sit on her feet in the chair seat. After rearranging the stretchy but slimly cut knit, she looked up to find Matt's amused masculine gaze on her. "Now I know how women's pants-suits came into being," she said in some embarrassment.

"I'm old-fashioned enough to prefer it the other way around. There's a time and a place for everything it seems to me. Women should stick to skirts."

"That's your final decision on the subject?" she teased.

"Absolutely. You were going to tell me what the sheriff said."

She nodded. "The victim was a naturalized Canadian subject. Apparently he was involved in some minor offense in Italy a few years ago and later was arrested in Montreal on suspicion of transporting narcotics."

"Narcotics!" Matt's eyes lost their considering look and he sat bolt upright. "That's one I hadn't thought about." He frowned suddenly. "Did they say anything about the European clothing?"

"Only that passport agencies didn't have any record of recent European trips for him. So if he was in Italy last year, it must have been on a forged passport."

"Probably with that previous criminal record, he wasn't anxious to attract any attention when he was traveling."

She nodded agreement. "If he was in Italy," she repeated, stressing the first word. "For all we know, he could have Italian relatives supplying him with his clothes."

"Or he could have picked them up at the local thrift shop," Matt's lips twisted in a slanted smile. "But from appearances, I don't think he did. Was there any evidence that the man was an addict himself?"

She shook her head. "The sheriff said there was nothing to indicate he'd ever used heroin or anything similar. No needle marks, no physical evidence of drugs in the body at the time of death. The general consensus is that he was transporting or selling drugs rather than using them."

"If that's so, I wonder what he was doing at the Killara turnoff?" His gaze was focused on the park outside, but it was obvious that his thoughts were far from the peaceful scene.

She shifted in the chair and tugged futilely at her skirt again. "It could have been coincidence."

"Umm." He brought his attention back with a seeming effort. "There hasn't been any luck with witnesses who saw him around town?"

"Nary a one. For all the attention the man attracted, he might have dropped from the sky. He neither ate nor slept where any of the natives caught a glimpse of him. I understand the sheriff's men tried all the gas stations and tradesmen on both sides of the border but it was no go."

"I see." Matt's lighthearted air had completely evaporated and he looked suddenly weary, the lines at the corners of his eyes deepened in thought. "Well," his tone was deliberate, "there isn't anything we can do about it from here, so let's forget it for the time being."

"I'm in favor of that." She tried to restore his good humor. "Actually, I'm a total loss on mysteries anyhow. The last time I was in London, I couldn't even find my way out of the Hampton Court maze . . . the gateman had to come and rescue me."

"That's hardly the way to keep up our national image. No wonder we have such trouble with foreign relations. And speaking of those," he glanced again at his watch and rose hurriedly, "I'd better get going. I'm late for a meeting now. Unfortunately, there's a trustee's dinner tonight. I can't get out of that, but since tomorrow's Sunday, we'll have all the time in the world."

"Time for what?"

"To play." He picked up the slide case and moved toward the door. "Lord, it will be nice to have a whole day free. I think I'll start it by taking you out to breakfast." He paused with his hand on the doorknob. "Does that appeal to you?"

"It sounds marvelous," she admitted frankly. "You know, that's just what Jill hoped you would do."

"What? Take you out to breakfast?" He was amused.

"Of course not." She tried to make her voice severe. "She was worried that you were working too hard and didn't have time to relax."

"I'll reform then." His look was intent upon her. "You can be part of my cure."

Diana dropped her gaze in confusion. This was going too fast for comfort; better to bring the conversation back to safer territory. "You won't forget to send up the notes and typewriter later this afternoon, will you? I still feel as if I'm here under false pretenses."

"If you insist on being a drudge." The grin that took years off his age had reappeared. Even the dark-rimmed glasses didn't look as professorial as usual. "Better have some lunch and then take another nap until you catch up on your sleep."

"Sleep all afternoon . . ." her expression was horrified ". . . when I have a brand-new paycheck in my pocket and free time in London? You can't be serious!"

"You sound just like Jill." He opened the door. "Would you have time to find me a present for her?"

"Of course . . . as a consolation prize for missing the trip. Does she like anything special?"

"Most everything," he said dryly. "What do you suggest?"

"I've never known a woman who could resist a cashmere sweater," she offered tentatively.

"I'll remember that. Does it apply to you, as well?"

"We are not talking about me," she said. "I'll find her an elegant one in Knightsbridge. Have a good meeting and enjoy your dinner."

"Sure you can manage all right?"

Her smile was spontaneous. "In the vernacular of the country, I'll have a bash at it. You'd better be going . . ."

"I know." His glance flickered momentarily to her parted lips and then he gave her a mock salute. "Till tomorrow morning, then. I'll meet you down in the dining room at eight. If you're not there, I'll come and pound on your door."

"Don't worry . . . I'll be there."

She watched him go down the hall and disappear around the corner to the elevators before she closed her door softly. Leaning back against the panel, she shut her eyes as if she was suddenly afraid of what they might see. It was no use; there wasn't an escape from reality. Matthew wasn't just carrying away photographic slides in that leather case . . . he had taken her heart as well.

She could have acknowledged the truth of their relationship days before. There had been an acute awareness during the stay in the cabin; the ridiculous feeling of happiness when he had come down to the pasture fence to say good-bye, and now . . . now there had been the tremendous urge to put her arms around his shoulders and keep him with her always.

The fact that they had known each other scarcely a week had nothing to do with it. When had falling in love been measured by a standard of time? The only standard was her awareness that life without him would be hard to endure.

The real question was how Matt felt about her. She had no doubt that he found her reasonably attractive. A woman would have to be completely devoid of feelings not to recognize the spark that had flared between them. Tomorrow they would breakfast together, play together, and probably dine together. They would flirt, hold hands, and doubtless exchange a good-night kiss or two. But in less than a week they would be back in Killara and if her typing was satisfactory, she would rank slightly behind Dr. Reynolds' palomino and a little ahead of his burro.

Not that Matt would ever intimate as much. She had been with him long enough by now to know that his true feelings would lie carefully beneath the veneer of impeccable manners. Even Jill had warned of this.

Diana walked slowly over to the window and stared down at the velvety green of Hyde Park. There was a reluctance to admit falling in love, even to oneself. When the spark was hidden, it could be nourished and protected but if it were brought out in the open ...

She watched the trees lining Park Lane bend in front of a sudden gust of wind and then straighten, their leaves still fluttering. Love could be fanned to a fire in the same way or extinguished just as fast so that not a smolder remained.

She closed her eyes wearily and leaned her forehead against the cool window glass. It would be better to clamp down on her heart's fluttering right now. Play it light ... play it easy. She hadn't reached the age of twenty-five without learning a few of the harder romantic lessons along the way. Laugh, love a little, and forget it ... then do it all over again next time. That was the only way.

Diana looked down to see her hands clenched so tightly that her nails were biting into her palms. The graceful fingers straightened slowly and then came up to shield her eyes, vainly trying to stem the tears that suddenly streamed down her cheeks.

Chapter Six

When Matt arrived in the dining room promptly at eight o'clock, he found Diana already ensconced at a round table with a cup of tea in front of her.

"Don't tell me I'm the late one; that's always been a feminine prerogative."

"Have a cup of coffee and stop fussing," she told him. "I'm sure you're dead on time, but I've been to an early church service."

"So that's the reason for all the elegance." He gave an approving glance to her brown polkadot silk sheath. A plain brown silk travel raincoat was folded over the back of her chair. "You look almost too bright-eyed for me. That trustees' dinner of mine went on and on until the small hours."

"With remarks about old Smythe-Thomas and whether he was going to make department head?"

"How did you know about that?" He accepted a steaming cup of coffee from a hovering waiter and made a grimace of distaste as he sipped it. "I could certainly make better coffee than this," he complained softly.

"Serves you right. You should have ordered tea."

"Not first thing in the morning." He pushed aside the coffee and gave her a penetrating glance. "I asked how you knew about Smythe-Thomas?"

"Don't tell me I was right!" A contagious giggle bubbled out. "I was just quoting Jill. She reported what went on at your starchy dinners."

"My sister talks too much," he said definitely but without rancor. "Have you ordered?"

She nodded. "Yes, thanks. They're holding it so we can eat together."

"Fine." He gave his order to the waiter who was standing attentively at his elbow and watched him thread his way toward the kitchen. "It's a good thing we know we're in London," he said absently.

"What do you mean?"

"There are so many continental waiters in this place that you practically have to use sign language," he complained. "That one was Italian, wasn't he?"

"I think so. Probably they're over here on some hotel employment exchange so they can learn English. You should have switched to your fluent Italian."

"I might be able to get through bacon and eggs in my halting Italian," he corrected, "but

I'd damned well draw a blank when it came to ordering toasted corn muffins."

"Now I know what to get for your birthday," she said solemnly. *"Handy Italian Phrases for the Traveler."*

He raised his eyebrows. "I can see the contents now. 'Mama mia, the pen of my aunt is in Napoli' or 'Waiter, where is the nearest tavola calda?' "

"You're dithering," she said in pleased surprise. "I didn't know a parasitologist could dither. It's like discovering that Albert Einstein liked to read comic books."

He picked up a spoon to eat the half grapefruit which had just been placed in front of him. "That's slander. Drink your orange juice and use your mind to think about what you want to do today."

"I thought you had the itinerary all planned." She kept her tone light, remembering her decision of the previous night. That way he'd never know that he'd collected a feminine scalp to hang at his belt without even having to fight for it.

Matt gave her a puzzled glance. "I have some idea, naturally, but I thought you'd have something special you wanted to see."

"You're very thoughtful," she said carefully. "Actually, I think we've accomplished the sightseeing you're supposed to do. I promise to raise a terrible fuss if you've planned anything like touring the pushcart stalls in Portobello Road."

"Fair enough, and I draw the line at window-shopping in Carnaby Street." He finished his grapefruit and pushed it aside. "It looks as if we've been lucky in the weather so we might stroll up through Hyde Park and see who's grousing at Marble Arch. Then, after the soapbox orators, we could meander through Knightsbridge. Is that enough to be going on with?"

"I couldn't have chosen better," she agreed happily. "When we finish breakfast, I'll dash up and change to some low-heeled shoes so I'll last the day."

"All right, but don't change anything else. I like you the way you are."

When he talked like that, Diana decided crossly, it made it terribly hard for a woman to stick to her resolutions.

He was still being the perfect companion later in the forenoon when they had wended their way to Knightsbridge and a shabby coffee house that Diana had discovered the day before.

The restaurant wasn't crowded and Matt let his long legs protrude under the adjoining table as he surveyed the dimly lit interior.

"Very nice," he decided. "Not a sign of stainless steel or chrome plating anywhere."

"That probably means no automatic dishwashers," Diana chided. "Aren't you afraid of picking up some horrible bug?"

"I know all about horrible bugs." His grin

was lopsided. "And you should know more than you did last week at this time. Incidentally, thanks for typing those notes last night. They look fine."

She leaned toward him to allow the waitress to put their coffee on the table in front of them and then sat back. "I'm glad they're all right. Strangely enough, I'm just beginning to realize how important the study of parasites can be."

"Don't put any halos around our heads. For the one bit of important research accomplished, most of us spend months sorting out extraneous material."

"I promise not to erect a single pedestal," she said. "And I'll have to admit that even with my advanced knowledge, the liver fluke and I will never be soulmates."

"I sincerely hope not. Let's see, sugar and no cream, isn't it? Want to try these coffee crystals?"

"Um-humm." She popped one in her mouth before sugaring her coffee. "I meant to get a box to take home when I was shopping yesterday. That reminds me . . . I found a wonderful cardigan for Jill in a watermelon pink that should be lovely with her hair."

"Such enthusiasm!" He took a sip of black coffee and leaned back to study her features. "All over the purchase of a sweater; no scientific mind in the budding, I'm afraid."

"You're right," she said deliberately. "I could

have told you before that we didn't have much in common."

His friendly expression stiffened as he digested her rebuff. "I didn't realize that you thought it was so important. Maybe women pay more attention to something like that than a man."

"Maybe we do." Her bright smile felt as if it had been pinned on and was badly in danger of slipping. She groped desperately for a change of subject. "We're being very serious all of a sudden. It must be this coffee . . . It really isn't very good, is it?"

"I hadn't noticed." He took another sip and pushed it away. "God awful . . . you warned me at breakfast too. Oh well, at least it was a chance to sit down. All that wandering around Hyde Park makes me realize I'm out of condition."

Diana was determined to recapture their earlier mood. "You're just discouraged because that last speaker at Marble Arch claimed the world was coming to an end."

His grin came back briefly. "I'd forgotten about that. The world's coming to an end and here we are sitting around grousing about a cup of coffee."

"Correction, Dr. Reynolds," she said severely, "you're grousing, I'm not. The way you're complaining about the food makes you sound like the prototype of an American tourist."

"I am an American tourist," he replied

131

calmly. "I also am a firm believer in giving credit where credit is due. For example, the English countryside has some magnificent scenery and their sense of historical pageantry puts the rest of the world to shame. On the other hand, their servings of cold toast and hunks of slab cake have probably set civilization back a hundred years."

She gave a low chuckle. "English tourists have their complaints, too. I met one in Chicago who told me quite seriously that America's domestic ills were caused by the miserable cottage cheese salads we consumed at every meal."

His eyes crinkled in amusement. "There's a legitimate cause for a protest movement. Much better than your orator who claimed the world was coming to an end because of air pollution."

"Even according to his timetable, we have a few months yet." She glanced at her watch. "But if we're going to make the most of this day, we'd better get cracking."

"Cracking is the operative word." He grimaced as he rubbed the back of his neck. "I feel as if I'd like to sleep for a week. I don't suppose I could interest you in sitting in the sun on a park bench with me," he asked hopefully.

"Not a chance," she said firmly. "You said that today was our day to play, and play we will."

"The oracle has spoken," he sounded

amused. "Very well. Lead on . . . but it's your turn to furnish the itinerary."

"All right." She watched him fish out some change to cover the bill and then slid her chair back. "First, I'll show you a clock store where I was shopping yesterday. It's right around the corner and I want to drool over something in the window. Then we can catch a bus practically in front of the store and ride out to Regent's Park."

"The zoo?" He looked intrigued as he held the door for her. "Are you a zoo buff, too?"

"One of the worst," she confessed. "Usually it's one of the first places I go, but I've never had time in London before. If you don't want to look at the animals, I'll find you a bench and let you get your nap over before I come back to collect you."

He took her hand and pulled it through the crook of his elbow as if it were the most natural thing in the world to do. "Don't be silly. You can't get rid of me that easily. We're not so far apart on some things as you think. I'm an old hand at the Regent's Park Zoo."

She gave him a dubious glance. "I'm beginning to think that's not the only thing you're an old hand at."

His hand tightened over hers. "You're a fresh wench too. Where's this clock shop you were talking about?"

"Right here." She pulled him to a stop in front of a tiny antique clock dealer's window

133

and peered into its dim recesses. "See that lovely old clock over there." She pointed to an oak mantel clock displayed in the corner. "I spent my time yesterday poring over it. It's a German chiming bracket clock . . ."

"Wait a minute . . . you've left me behind already. What do you mean by bracket clock?"

"That's what they call mantel clocks over here." She was so intent upon the window display that she missed his amused flicker of interest at her professional tone. "Just the way they say long case clocks instead of grandfather clocks."

"I see." His voice was grave. "And by chiming, you must mean that it sounds the Westminster every hour."

"Plus the Whittington and Winchester melody," she said enthusiastically, "in the most lovely rich chimes you've ever heard. Most of his stock are just striking clocks, where they sound one note on the quarter and the half. That one has the whole bag of tricks."

He smiled down at her. "You sound quite the expert on clocks. If you like that one so much, why don't you buy it?"

"Because it costs the earth," she said practically. "So much that if I bought it, I'd probably tell my boss in New York about it. The next time one of the firm's clients needed a special timepiece, he'd remind me of it. Then zip . . . no clock."

"But you'd make a profit on it, wouldn't

you?" he probed, watching her profile intently.

"I suppose so. But I wouldn't have the clock, would I? No," she shook her head firmly, "I swore I'd never do that again. I'd rather leave it here in the window and let somebody buy it who just plain loves it." She looked up at him as if suddenly aware of how long they had been standing there. "Forgive me, I didn't mean to bore you; I don't often get on my hobby horse." She looked down the street behind them. "Here comes the red rover that goes to the main gate of the zoo." She pointed to the big double-decker bus that was pulling up at Matt's signal. "It doesn't look a bit crowded."

He swung onto the back step beside her and pointed her toward the curving stair to the upper deck. "All the better for us. Let's go upstairs."

She clung to the rail as the bus lurched forward. "Are you game for the front seat if it's vacant?"

He put a steadying hand at her waist. "The front seat, by all means. Today, Miss Burke, I'm game for anything."

The front seat was vacant and they rode out to the park in a companionable silence broken only by an occasional comment as the bus passed something of interest.

They got down at the main gate of the zoo and Matt steered her across the busy street.

"Half a minute until I get the tickets," he told her.

"Do they charge admission to a zoo?"

"That's not unusual . . . San Diego does the same thing. Besides, this is a rare bargain."

"I'm sure you're right." She laughed suddenly. "I didn't know I was going to be such an expensive date."

"Think nothing of it." His gaze wasn't as casual as she would have liked. "I generally get my own back. Most men taking out an attractive woman plan on it. If worst comes to worst, there'll be an additional deduction on your paycheck."

"Listen to the man!" She watched him purchase two tickets and then walked beside him to the gate. "Your Aunt Violet forgot to warn me."

"I'm lucky she slipped up." He pushed her gently through the turnstile. "Which way?"

She was reading the direction signs. "Do you feel for bears, giraffes, or what?"

"Mainly what." He turned her down one of the paved paths thronged with English families. Most of the women pushed prams in front of them and their husbands trailed dogs on leashes beside them. "If you haven't been here before," Matt went on, "you'll have to pay a visit to their giant panda . . . the famous Chi-Chi."

"Of course!" She turned an enthusiastic face up to him. "I've read about her. One of the two pandas in the Western world, isn't she?"

"I think so. The other one is a male in the

Moscow zoo. He's been a house guest here by invitation several times but so far, no baby pandas."

"Love didn't conquer all," she murmured.

"Let's say that love didn't conquer Chi-Chi. The flower beds are pretty, aren't they?"

"Perfectly marvelous. Look . . ." she tugged at his arm, "there's the penguin moat. I have to see it."

She stood on tiptoe and peered over the concrete wall to see at least a dozen brown and white penguins standing solemnly next to a shallow pool of water. Another half-dozen were waddling importantly around the edge to join them.

"Aren't they wonderful!" Diana exclaimed. "Almost too perfect to be real. Wasn't it John Ruskin who said that whenever he felt unhappy, he went to the zoo and looked at the penguins? Just think . . . maybe he came here to Regent's Park."

"We can hope he did, anyway," Matt agreed as they turned to stroll on down the path. "He certainly had the right idea. Zoos are marvelous for raising anybody's morale. I remember visiting the zoo in Colombo, Ceylon, where they had the most wonderful elephant act I've ever seen. After the show, they invited us behind the scenes to view their newest arrival. He was a baby elephant just about two feet high and when he wound his miniature trunk around your finger, you wanted to bundle him up and take him home. I'll bet he had more godparents than royalty."

"What fun! I wish I'd been there to see him." She tucked her purse more securely under her arm. "You know, you're not what I imagined a professor to be at all."

"Should I be discreet and say a change of topic is indicated at this point?" he asked teasingly.

"Stop humoring me," she protested. "That's what I mean . . . I thought I was going out West to decorate for some stodgy and fusty scientist. One who never moved except to go from one textbook to another. You know the type; all they ever say is, 'This thesis is not acceptable, Armstrong' or 'Your semester marks are going to reflect your lack of ambition, Caruthers.'"

He burst out laughing. "Diana . . . you couldn't have been more outdated. Professors don't talk like that."

"Mine did," she assured him. "That's why I couldn't wait to get away from them."

"Well, I'm glad that you've admitted me to the human race." He shoved his hands in the pockets of his gray flannel slacks as they sauntered along the path. "Sometimes I've felt the ten years' difference in our ages more than you know."

She stared up at him in amazement. "I can't imagine why."

"You mean you don't?"

"Of course not." Her tone was definite but

her eyes dropped before his sidelong glance. "Age has nothing to do with the way people look at things." There was a short silence before she went on, "Do you suppose I'll be tempting cloudy weather if I put on my dark glasses?"

"Probably. You don't need them. Here's Chi-Chi's cage . . . it looks as if you're going to have to hunt through the long grass for her."

"Oh darn!" She pressed up against the bars of the cage. "Look, there she is over in the far corner. You can just see a lump of something white."

"Umm. Probably a goodly section of her derriere," he said dryly and fished a sixpence from his pocket. "Go put this in that talking machine hanging on the post and learn about the other parts of Chi-Chi's anatomy."

She put on the headphones with docility and listened to the recorded spiel. At the conclusion, she put the ear piece on the receiver, gave Chi-Chi's recumbent figure a farewell glance, and rejoined Matt on the walk.

"Do you know everything about pandas now?" he asked, taking her hand absently and strolling on.

"I'm a gold mine of the last-minute information," she said rather breathlessly, trying to disregard the unsettled feeling that his nearness gave her. "Did you know that there are English Boy Scouts in the midlands who spend most of their time gathering tender bamboo shoots for Chi-Chi's dinner?"

"God protect me from the female mind!"

"Don't be disrespectful. It was just that hearing about Chi-Chi's dinner reminded me of food. Since I have no intention of letting you get away with feeding me a cheap meal at the zoo, we could start walking back."

"A designing female mind at that . . . the worst kind." He stopped to look at a group of direction signs. "Nothing on here about the burro pasture. It's a pity . . . we could have gone and looked at Carmen's sisters and her cousins and her brothers and her aunts."

"I believe you're fond of that moth-eaten creature," she murmured indistinctly.

"Of course I am. Carmen has real charisma," he said. "Those stained, yellow teeth of hers add a great deal too. . . ."

"Stop it, idiot! There may be more bedraggled-looking burros around, but I haven't seen one. She's the only living being I've ever seen who looks better after rolling in the mud." She paused. "Where are we headed now?"

They were at the top of a flight of steps leading to a boat landing which abutted a twenty-foot-wide canal filled with dark, slow-moving water. A launch with a canvas canopy was tied to the wharf, its double row of seats almost filled with patrons.

"We're on our way home," he said, pulling her gently forward, "aboard a zoo water-taxi. The English equivalent of a rowboat in Central Park." He helped her into a seat by the stern.

"Professor or not . . . you are inspired." She gazed in delight as a young crewman casually cast off the bow line and the ancient craft edged slowly forward with a muted roar of the asthmatic motor. There was a footpath along the canal's sloping banks which was occupied at intervals by young fishermen or couples strolling hand-in-hand.

"It's like being a million miles away from the city, isn't it?" she said as trees formed an almost complete bower overhead.

"We'll be back soon," he warned. "It's a short trip."

"Then I intend to enjoy every foot of it. What was it you said when you took me back to Killara after the night in the cabin . . . 'belt up and let me think?' "

"Surely nothing so inelegant," he protested, but he smiled as he said it and firmly tucked her hand in his jacket pocket.

It really didn't matter if the boat sank, Diana reflected in a sudden haze of happiness. The way she was feeling, she could have walked on water all the way down to the Thames and never gotten her feet wet.

It was late afternoon when they finally strolled across Park Lane and into the lobby of the hotel.

"I've made a dinner reservation for six-thirty," Matt told her as they waited for an elevator. "Does that give you time enough to do whatever you want?"

141

She pushed a strand of hair back into place and laughed up at him. "The main thing I want to do is get into a tub of lovely hot water and submerge. I'm wearing a top layer of London grime."

He flipped a casual finger at the end of her nose as he pretended to survey it. "I like you this way. All that New York gloss has worn off . . . amazing what was underneath."

An elevator arrived and they stepped into it. The automatic door closed quickly behind them giving them the entire cubicle to themselves.

"Does your gloss ever wear away, Dr. Reynolds?"

Matt pressed the button for her floor. "There's no gloss there, Miss Burke." He put solemn emphasis on her surname. "Rough and ragged edges throughout. Comes from having been raised in a wickiup."

"Were you really? I didn't know . . ." her voice trailed off as she saw the spark of amusement in his eyes. "Foxed again! You'd think I'd eventually catch on when I'm being led down the garden path."

The elevator stopped at her floor and she paused halfway through the door. "Getting back to dinner . . . six-thirty will be fine. Where shall I meet you?"

"I'll probably be ordering a dry martini in the lounge on the second floor, so it won't matter if you're a little late. All right with you?"

"Very much so. I'll see you then." She stepped out of the elevator and gave him a brief wave as the doors slid smoothly together.

The bath worked wonders for her morale. So did the coral chiffon dinner dress with a knife-pleated skirt which blended so beautifully with an autumn haze stole. A discreet dab of Worth's *"Vers Toi"* on her ear lobes and the inside of her elbows made her feel as if she had done her best in the cause of femininity. The smothered whistle of a passing page boy as she waited for the elevator added the final fillip of approval to her ensemble.

Her heels sank into the deep carpet on the second floor as she hesitated in the doorway of the cocktail lounge. Matt, elegant in a black dinner jacket, straightened from his lounging position at the end of the bar. His glance swept over her as he came swiftly to her side.

"You look marvelous," he said in a quiet voice. "If I had the talent, I'd start spouting poetry."

She smiled up at him. "Not that," she protested, striving to keep her voice level. "One of the nicest things about you is that you've skipped the 'Diana—chaste and fair' bit."

He took her elbow and led her to the adjoining dining room. "So my sins of omission are finally paying dividends? It's about time. Let's have our drinks at the table, shall we?"

She followed a dining room captain to a table for two by the long windows.

Once they were seated and frosty martini glasses were in front of them Matt continued. "I hope you don't mind being shepherded in here. Bars are always too noisy and too dark."

She shook her head as she nibbled on her green olive. "It's much nicer here. What a marvelous dining room!" She gave him a suddenly suspicious glance. "Aren't you supposed to be doing something with the conference?"

He reddened slightly. "Everybody's entitled to skip a few things now and then. Besides, I didn't come over here for the social side and the rest of it has gone by the boards. There are some interviews I should conduct in the next day or so, but otherwise I'm a free agent." He took up the long menu. "Anything special you want to eat?"

She shook her head. "You decide, providing it isn't hamburger or caviar."

"You do run the gamut. By the same token, I'll wash out snails and peanut butter." He perused the bill of fare and then nodded to the white-coated waiter who was watching from a discreet distance. "We'll try something a little more middle-of-the-road."

To Diana's mind that was a prosaic description for the prawn cocktails and the succulent chicken Kiev that followed. Much later, she waved away the dessert cart loaded with pastries and trifles to settle simply for coffee.

"It was all delicious," she breathed. "I'll

never say another nasty word about English cooking. But the calories!"

"Remember Thoreau? He had the right idea."

"What was that?"

"Something about only dieting between meals. Besides . . ." once again that warm glance of his slid swiftly over her, "it's obvious that you don't have to worry."

"It's when you stop worrying that you'd better start," she said darkly.

He shook his head. "Deliver me from feminine reasoning. Now—about the rest of the evening . . ."

She was destined not to hear the rest of his plans, for just then she felt a hard, masculine arm go around her shoulders and a melting Italian voice in her ear.

"Diana . . . *amante* . . . why didn't you tell me you were in London?"

She couldn't have answered if she'd tried because she was being kissed in a positive manner that made her struggle for breath. She noted hazily that Matt had shot to his feet in amazement.

Protestingly, she put her hands against a ruffled shirt front and pushed back to see an unexpectedly familiar face. Ordinarily, it would have brought her to her feet cheering, but seeing the storm clouds gather over Matt Reynolds' stern features she could only gasp, "Carlo . . . what on earth are you doing here?"

The newcomer, who was broad-shouldered

and an extraordinarily handsome man in his early thirties, shook his head in mock sorrow.

"What a way to greet your dearest!" He turned to Matt and became serious. "A thousand apologies, *signore*. Evidently my arrival has made the little one forget her manners. I'm Carlo Mangini and I met Diana some months ago when she stayed with my mother in Trieste."

And that should bring the walls tumbling down, Diana thought.

It did. Matt's face froze. "I'm Matt Reynolds . . . a business acquaintance of Miss Burke. Won't you join us?"

"*Grazie, signore*." Carlo sank into the chair which a dining room captain promptly and unobtrusively provided. "If you're sure I won't be interrupting anything."

"Certainly not." Matthew couldn't have been more definite.

Diana leaned forward. "I still don't understand what you're doing in London, Carlo."

"It's just a stopover, *carina*. Actually, I'm on my way to the States. I was going to call you when I got to New York."

"Then it's fortunate we met in London because I've been assigned to the West Coast to do a job for Dr. Reynolds."

Carlo smote his forehead in a theatrical gesture. "Now you tell me. My dear Diana, you should keep me up to date with an occasional letter. Mamma has been asking about you."

"Carlo's family has a hotel in Trieste," Diana said hurriedly to Matt. "Mrs. Mangini was perfectly wonderful to me when I did some decorating for them."

"Mamma fell in love with you," Carlo broke in, "just as all the rest of us did." He turned to Matt. "I'm sure I don't need to tell you how talented she is."

"Certainly not, but I hadn't realized her fame was so internationally recognized," Matt answered tersely.

Diana winced at the implications of his remark. "It's not," she said. "Carlo is just being nice."

"No . . . no, she's marvelous," Carlo protested, his English skill not sufficiently acute to appreciate Matt's sarcastic overtones. "Only in one thing does she need improvement . . . that's with the horses. Is this still so, *carissima*?"

Despite herself, Diana giggled. "More than ever, Carlo. Dr. Reynolds' sister has been giving me instruction and she made the same comments about my flapping elbows that you did."

Matt's expression softened slightly. "You didn't tell me."

"It certainly wasn't worth bragging about." She pushed her coffee cup away. "Carlo should meet Jill."

"This Miss Jill . . . she likes horses?"

The beam on Carlo's face made Matt relent still more. "Very much," he said. "Too much, probably. If you get out to our neighborhood, you must drop in. My ranch is close to the Canadian border—just south of Vancouver. Diana can tell you how to get there."

"You are kind." The Italian's gaze sharpened suddenly. "Now that is a . . . what do you call it, Diana . . . when fate seems to come in?"

"Coincidence?"

"Si . . . coincidence. Vancouver is one of my stops. I have an uncle there and the family has given me some business to transact."

"The Manginis are quite a family," Diana explained. "Carlo is a lawyer and his younger brother serves on a committee of the World Health Organization."

"Fortunately, my elder brother likes the hotel business," Carlo put in, "so we can indulge in our various careers and still eat regularly." He sat back and beamed on them impartially. "But this is wonderful! I was going to ask Diana to come back to Italy and stay with us some months: Now perhaps I can have the opportunity of seeing your home as well, Dr. Reynolds."

"I'll look forward to it," Matt told him quietly. Glancing at his watch he said, "I must get on up to my room. The hotel operator told me that an overseas call has been booked to come through about this time."

"Do you suppose anything has happened to Jill?" Diana asked.

"I doubt it." Matt idly traced a design on the tablecloth with the handle of his coffee spoon.

"She should be in the midst of the Canadian wedding party about now. There could be some news of Killara, though. My foreman has been instructed to keep in touch with me if anything comes up," he told Carlo. "We had some unpleasantness there recently . . . something about dope smuggling over the border."

Carlo pursed his lips thoughtfully. "I understand authorities are having difficulties with that all over the world; they certainly do in northern Italy. In Trieste, we are so close to the Mideast sources of supply that our law enforcement people have great problems."

"I remember Alfonso telling about it when I was staying with your mother," Diana said.

"*Si.* My younger brother Alfonso works with such things," he explained to Matt. Turning to Diana, he continued hesitantly, "Would I be intruding if I stayed with you while Dr. Reynolds is taking his telephone call?"

Diana looked over at Matt, unsure of his reaction. It wasn't long in coming.

"Of course not," he said, signaling to the waiter for the dinner check. "I know you have a lot to tell Diana . . ."

"That certainly," Carlo broke in. "It may be that we will even be able to go to Vancouver on the same plane. My family would like to have her back this winter and I'm afraid this may take much persuading."

"I see." There was a wealth of irony in Matt's

words. "Well, if that's so, I'll leave you to get on with it."

"In my case," Carlo assured him earnestly, "Diana will not be the huntress of mythology. I must reverse the procedure."

"Ah, yes, renowned Diana 'chaste and fair.'" Matt's tall form hovered over the table. "There's another side to the coin, though. According to legend, it was Diana who attracted plagues and sudden death." His eyes, as they looked down at her, were as bleak as a north wind. "Good night, Mr. Mangini . . . good-bye, Miss Burke."

And that, thought Diana, brings me right back to square one.

As she watched Matthew Reynolds' disappearing back, it was evident that the die was cast. The tangible proof didn't come until the next morning with a note slid under her hotel room door. The memory of another note under the door at Killara came to mind as she stooped to pick up the white, folded paper. She carried it back by the windows to read and sank onto the arm of a nearby chair before she had gotten past the first sentence.

"Dear Miss Burke" . . . Matt's broad script was forceful and Diana was well aware that the formal salutation had been penned quite deliberately. Now that Carlo had arrived on the scene, she had once again become an entity to be treated with formality and from a safe distance. As she read on, she became sickeningly aware of just how great that distance was to be. "By the time you read this, I will be on a flight back home. The latest word from Killara has convinced me that I should return as soon as possible. As you have just arrived in London, it seems unnecessary to change your plans as well. Please feel free to return at your convenience. All arrangements have been made regarding the occupancy of your hotel room. If you should care to alter your return plans to fit those of Mr. Mangini, I shall, of course, understand. Best wishes, Matthew Reynolds."

If he had written it on parchment and wrapped it in purple ribbons, he couldn't have said good-bye more decisively. Matthew had simply taken one look at the opposition and withdrawn from the field. There hadn't been a battle, not even a skirmish.

The only thing he had overlooked was a sedan chair for carrying her listless body to the triumphant Italian conqueror.

Chapter Seven

Where the overcast sky at Heathrow had been gray and streaming, the weather conditions at Vancouver's international airport looked like an advertisement for the Good Humor man. Bright sunlight beamed down on the busy runways and infiltrated deplaning passengers with the feeling that on such a marvelous day God must be in his heaven and all had to be right with the world.

Carlo sniffed the clean, fresh air with an appreciative nose. "This is a beautiful place. I'm glad you persuaded me to come."

"I persuaded you!" Diana pulled her silk travel coat over her arm and nodded a polite good-bye to the hostess standing by the front exit of the plane. "Somehow the story has changed in the translation. What about your uncle?" She shot a suddenly suspicious glance at him as he followed her into the terminal. "You do have an uncle in Vancouver, don't you?"

"Diana . . . of course! You've heard my

mamma speak of Uncle Bruno."

She surveyed the group of people waiting to greet the passengers from their flight. "Then why," she asked, "isn't he here to meet you?"

"Probably because I didn't call to let him know I was arriving," he told her patiently. "An omission which I will remedy right now, if you'll wait for me."

"Of course," she gave him a sheepish smile. "Forgive my bad temper."

"Certainly, *cara mia*." He squeezed her elbow gently. "I am sorry that you are so distrait these days. You must be working too hard. I wish I could persuade you to come back and spend some months with us. No . . ." he held up an admonishing hand, "don't worry, I promised not to say any more on the subject and I will keep my word . . . for now."

"Carlo, my dear . . ." Her voice was soft and, for the moment, they were unaware of the hurrying crowds of people around them in the terminal. "Nothing has changed. I'm sorry but that's the way it is." She gave a slight shrug as if to indicate how inarticulate she had become. "I wish I were in love with you. The woman who becomes your wife will have the nicest husband in the world and inherit the most marvelous family in Italy." She pressed her gloved hand on his sleeve. "You're all far too fine to ever settle for second best."

Carlo's usually pleasant expression became bleak as he listened to her words. "So the best

153

thing is to put it out of my mind, eh? Is that what you think?" He gave a Latin shrug. "I promise to try, Diana."

"In that case," her tone was lighthearted with an effort, "you'd better go and call your Uncle Bruno. But don't forget that I'm expecting you to take me out for some pasta before I go south."

Diana watched him stride toward the phone booths and walked idly over to survey the gift shop windows.

The past days in London and the flight across Canada had been redeemed solely by Carlo's good humor. He hadn't commented on Matt's abrupt departure more than to say the other's ill luck couldn't help but be his good fortune. Then he had promptly whirled Diana off into a round of Mayfair activities that had amused and exhausted her. There was a handful of Mangini relatives in London plus a barrelful of their friends and the bountiful Italian hospitality had been unstinted.

During that time, she had done her best to put Matt's terse note in the background but failed miserably. Lacerated pride demanded that she ask David Royle for another commission while common sense dictated that it would be a Pyrrhic victory. Torn between the two, she had felt like a ghost at the feast despite her determined efforts to the contrary.

If she were to take Matt's farewell note strictly at face value, then the trip West had been strictly for scenery. On the other hand, if their Sunday in London meant anything to him, she could at least make one more effort to salvage her heart's desire. It seemed obvious that he had gotten the wrong end of the stick so far as Carlo was concerned; he had taken effusive Italian phrases and manner to indicate a betrothal.

If she could only have explained. She made a wry grimace at her reflection in the shop window. Fancy getting Matthew Reynolds to believe such an explanation. He would listen quietly with that frozen expression of his and then tell her politely that he didn't believe a word of it.

She rested her forehead momentarily against the cool glass. The best she could hope for was an interlude of status quo in which to pick up some of the broken pieces. At least Matt wasn't apt to throw her out on her ear; he still needed a secretary to type those darned notes of his.

"Diana . . . here you are! Thank heavens, I thought I'd missed you."

She turned to see Jill bearing down on her with a relieved expression on her face.

"I didn't expect you," Diana told her happily as she was caught up in an enthusiastic bear hug. "Are you by yourself?" She tried to see if there were a tall, masculine figure hovering without being obvious about it.

Fortunately Jill was blithely unaware. "For the moment. Jim shared a taxi with me part of

155

the way. He said to tell you hello and that he'll see you later today."

"Fine." The disappointment in Diana's voice was well hidden. "It was marvelous of you to come but I really didn't expect it. When I sent you a telegram, I was just gently preparing you for my appearance at Killara. I had planned to rent a car later today and drive down."

"What an expense account Mr. Royle must give you!" Jill shook her head in mock disapproval. "You already have one car sitting in our garage. What in the world are you doing . . . collecting them?" Her chuckle was infectious. "I can hear Matt's disgusted comments now!"

"Is Matt home then?"

Jill's suddenly raised eyebrows indicated that the hopeful tone had not passed unnoticed. "Of course. He even arrived in time for the wedding reception. It was handy for me; I had two presentable men in tow."

"Two?"

"Uh-huh. Jim was in town, too. He's going through a few more tests at the hospital here as an out-patient."

Diana frowned in bewilderment. "I thought there was some crisis at Killara that brought your brother back."

"There was no crisis that I know of. At least, Matt didn't say anything."

"And there's nothing new that's happened?"

"Nothing startling. Jim heard from one of the

men that someone had tried to make off with a few head of our cattle. Fortunately, a couple of neighboring ranchers saw him."

"What happened?"

Jill shrugged. "The last they saw was the dust behind his empty truck as it disappeared down the road. The cattle are now back with the herd."

"It sounds like a television epic."

Jill shook her head blandly. "That's old-hat stuff. At least he didn't shoot the beef first and then say he thought the poor things were deer or elk. When hunting season comes, any stray cattle still out on the range should wear a scarlet ribbon tied to their tails."

"I can see you tying them on. There's nothing new on the murder, then?"

"Not unless there's a last-minute item Matt hasn't told me about. He's had all sorts of conferences and telephone calls since he's been back, but evidently a kid sister doesn't rate his confidence." She stared at Diana deliberately. "What happened in London, anyway?"

"What do you mean?"

"Just that. Talk about coming home with a sore head . . . brrr." Jill turned up her jacket collar and huddled inside it for emphasis. "I've had the original frozen mitt ever since. Matt was barely pleasant at the reception, which disconcerted an old flame of his. I think she'd been hoping for a weekend invitation to Killara."

157

Diana decided to play it carefully. "And it was no go?"

"The way Matt was behaving, he would have told Brigitte Bardot to try and make it later in the summer."

"I see." She smiled faintly. "What did he say happened in London?"

"Practically nothing," Jill told her blithely, "that's what makes me suspicious. Matt always clams up when something interesting happens. When I asked about you, he told me in about ten words that you had met an old Italian flame." She peered at Diana like a bright-eyed child. "Just how old and how warm a flame?"

Diana's laughter bubbled up. "You are an idiot! Not very and pretty cool, if you want it that way. Take a look for yourself . . . he's coming toward us right now."

"Di! Do you mean it?" Jill twisted her head to peer over her shoulder. "Not that gorgeous black-haired creature trying to gain yardage through the tour group?"

"That's the one," Diana said. "Hello Carlo . . . I was beginning to think you'd gotten lost."

Carlo was shaking his head ruefully. "No, but what a line at the telephones!"

"That's a shame. Jill, this is Carlo Mangini, my friend from Trieste." She tucked her hand under his elbow fondly. "I told you about him when we were out riding. Carlo . . . this is Dr. Reynolds' sister Jill."

"Of course, I remember." Jill put out her

hand spontaneously and Carlo held it for a moment as if he were too dazzled to be aware of what was happening. "Diana told me what a wonderful horseman you are," she went on.

"You are very kind," he stammered.

Diana was amused by his discomfiture. It wasn't often that Carlo's impeccable continental manners were thrown out of kilter. Jill's slim blond beauty evidently had caught him completely unaware.

"Carlo was planning to visit his uncle in Vancouver," she explained, "and was nice enough to keep me company on the plane across!"

"That isn't quite the way of it." Carlo had recovered his aplomb. "I was hoping to visit Diana in the States anyway, so this was a bonus. Dr. Reynolds mentioned you," he fixed Jill with a flattering stare, "when I met him in London. He was so kind as to ask me to call in at your home if I were in the area."

"What a marvelous idea!" Jill was incapable of dissimulation and gave him a sparkling smile. "You're certainly in the neighborhood and we'll be going back to Killara tomorrow."

"Tomorrow?" Diana was puzzled by her announcement. "Why not today?"

"I didn't have a chance to tell you. Matt said to go shopping today and spend the night up here. I already have our hotel room."

"Then let me offer you my taxi downtown," Carlo insisted, taking each of them by the elbow and steering them toward the entrance.

"I've taken care of the luggage and the cab is waiting by the door."

"Did you reach your uncle?" Diana asked.

He nodded. "Everything is arranged; I am to go out to his home and leave my luggage and then see him later on." He turned to Jill. "The address is near Park Royal in West Vancouver. Is that nearby?"

"Not far from downtown," she assured him as she got into the cab. "Fortunately, you'll be going right past our hotel in the central business district."

"You see, it was ordained," Carlo told her, smiling. He gave Diana a hand into the car and then pulled down a jump seat for himself.

Jill gave the driver the name of their hotel and the car moved off.

"Now let me get this settled in my mind," Carlo said as the taxi left the airport drive and joined the fast-moving traffic going into town. "You are both going to be in Vancouver tonight . . . is that right?"

Jill nodded again. "Matt insisted that this would be a good time for me to get my shopping spree over so that I can get to work when I'm home. I told him it wasn't necessary but he overruled me." She looked at them in mock dismay. "It's the first time I've ever known him to be so solicitous about my spending money. Usually he's bringing the roof down because I've overspent my allowance."

"Did he know I was arriving today?" Diana asked quietly.

"Oh, yes," Jill said, "he opened the telegram."

Diana winced inwardly. While she hadn't expected Matt to be in attendance, it was heartbreaking that he was going out of his way to avoid her.

"I have a suggestion," Carlo broke into the silence. "Perhaps you both would be my guests for dinner and the evening."

Jill looked slightly flustered. "It's kind of you and Diana to include me in your party . . ."

"Just a minute," Diana interrupted. "Carlo's invitation is news to me. We hadn't made any plans for the evening because I thought I'd be on my way south."

"This will be much better," Carlo assured them. "I can see my uncle in the afternoon and arrange to have the evening free."

"It sounds grand," Jill said and then clapped her hand to her mouth. "Oh . . . I'd forgotten!"

"What?" Diana asked.

"Jim. Jim Dodge, our foreman," Jill explained for Carlo's benefit. "I invited him to dinner. Matt asked me to keep him company . . . he said that he needed cheering up."

"I understand," Carlo said politely, then his face brightened. "Would it be all right if you and Jim joined Diana and me? We could still have our party . . . only now we have even numbers for dancing, no?"

"Yes!" Jill's eyes gleamed with excitement. "What do you say, Di?"

"Very nice. We'll spend all our money when we go shopping this afternoon and let our escorts pick up our dinner check this evening."

Carlo shook his head sorrowfully. "My mamma warned me to look out for such women."

"Don't listen to him, Jill," Diana scoffed. "His mother told me that she felt sorry for all the poor women Carlo and his brothers led astray."

Jill smiled. "That sounds more like the true story. Where did you learn to speak English so well, Mr. Mangini?"

"Carlo, please," he begged. "Then I can have a proper excuse for using your Christian name." He glanced toward Diana. "You see, *carina*—other people think my English is all right." He turned back to Jill. "Diana teases me because I went to school in England and I'm not sure of the latest American expressions. You'll have to teach me the new ones so I can go home and impress my family."

"I'm not sure that I know any," Jill confessed. "I'm too ancient to keep up on them, but if you'll come down and visit Killara, our young housemaid will fill you in."

"Good, I'll combine pleasure with research. Now you must get to work; this is my first visit

162

to Vancouver so please let me have the quick city tour."

Jill made a face. "So I have to work for my dinner! Very well, but it's on your own head."

The fairly short taxi ride limited Jill's sight-seeing lecture and they were soon pulling up in the curved entranceway of a modern hotel. Carlo helped them out of the car while the driver retrieved Diana's bags from the trunk. As the luggage was borne inside by a bellman, Carlo shook hands and told them that he would telephone from the lobby promptly at seven.

Jill watched his cab disappear into the crowded street before looking at Diana and sighing dramatically. "If Italy is full of handsome things like that, what have I been doing in this part of the world for so long?"

"Certainly not wasting away from a shortage of admirers," Diana chided. "This looks like a very elegant hotel. Take me up to our room and let me wash off the travel stains; you may not be enthusiastic about going shopping, but it sounds wonderful to me!"

"All right . . . but how you can think of stores when there's someone like Carlo around I don't understand . . . obviously you don't appreciate him. I promise not to poach," a solemn hand was raised, "because I don't think I'd have a chance." She guided Diana toward the elevators. "I've already registered for you, so we can go right up."

It was when they were in their spacious twin-bedded room and Diana had partially unpacked that she reverted to their former conversation.

"You wouldn't be poaching, you know," she said as she sank into a chair by the window overlooking Vancouver's Grouse Mountain.

It was a testimony to Jill's thoughts that she understood at once.

"You mean it?" She turned from the dressing table mirror. "That wasn't the way Matt understood the situation. He said Carlo was practically setting the date."

So Matthew *had* gone off hearing wedding bells. Diana's spirits took a cautious bound as she shook her head. "Never listen to a brother. He's got a little bit right and a lot more wrong. There's nothing secret about it; Carlo knows I'm very fond of him. Full stop. That's all there is or ever will be."

"Don't tell me Carlo approves of that state of affairs," Jill said shrewdly. "You should see the way he looks at you."

"Take that with a little salt. I wasn't fooling when I said the Mangini men could coax the birds from the trees." She ran a hand through her hair wearily. "Carlo can't help being charming to any attractive woman—it's sheer reflex action. At heart, though, he was a strictly European attitude toward wives."

"Is that bad?"

"Certainly not ... for Europeans," Diana

said carefully. "American women have been brought up to consider some values differently."

Jill chuckled. "You sound like a marriage counselor. All right, Di, I'm not about to lose my heart and soul to your 'charming continental.'"

"Well, don't lose your soul, anyway. It's hard not to lose a little bit of your heart. Carlo knows all the right things to say and dances divinely."

"In that case, I insist that we share the wealth tonight. On a dance floor, Jim moves as if he's rounding up strays."

Diana went over to the bed to retrieve her purse. "We can't have everything. Are you sure he'll feel up to socializing? Perhaps his doctor has him on strict orders."

"If he has, Jim isn't taking him very seriously. He tried to feed me a cocktail before lunch yesterday, and that's not on an ulcer diet."

"It certainly isn't. Well, we can ask him tonight." Diana closed her purse. "I'm all ready to go. Do we tour the department stores together or do you just want to point out the general area?"

Jill walked over to the closet and shrugged into a suede jacket. "We can start together and then separate later if we run out of steam."

They stayed together in the stores until mid-afternoon and finally arranged to meet back in their hotel room. Jill had decided to take a cab to West Vancouver to visit a tack shop and Diana headed toward the Chinese section of the city to see what was available in Oriental decor. Pender Street brought her into the international district and she walked slowly, enjoying the unusual food shops and curio stores. She was so intent upon her window-gazing that she wasn't aware of how the neighborhood had deteriorated until she heard angry masculine voices coming from a seamy corner tavern. Hurriedly, she moved into the entranceway of a nearby shop to get out of the way as the quarrel approached the front of the bar. There was a brief scuffle on the sidewalk and more harsh words in a guttural foreign tongue before the two participants eyed each other balefully and finally stalked off in opposite directions.

Diana peered gingerly over her shoulder at the man striding quickly down the far side of the street and then stared openly at his disappearing back. He was dressed in rough clothes with a greasy cap pushed back on his head, and Diana stood amazed, as she watched him out of sight. Then her senses returned in full measure. What on earth was Carlo Mangini doing in a tavern brawl in western Canada?

She turned back the way she had come, her glazed expression attracting mild curiosity from passersby.

It didn't seem possible that Carlo would appear in such surroundings, but there was no doubt of her identification. The tavern was another puzzle. While Carlo liked his wine as much as most Europeans, her stay with the Mangini family proved that he wasn't a compulsive alcoholic.

She bit her lip in concentration as she walked along. If Carlo wasn't in the tavern to satisfy any drinking desires, then he must have been there to meet someone. But why in the world would a successful Trieste lawyer be making such appointments in Canada? She shook her head as if to clear it. It wasn't the kind of question she could possibly ask him at the dinner table later in the evening. And from the rapid manner in which he left the neighborhood, he made it evident that he was not lingering for social chitchat.

Diana drew a hand across her forehead wearily. It was time to go back to the hotel so she'd better see if she could find a taxi to take her there. Luck was with her after a mercifully brief stand on a street corner. Then after a slightly longer journey through Vancouver's crowded one-way streets she once again reached the comfort of her hotel.

Jill, wrapped in a pink robe, poked her head around the bathroom door when she heard Diana's key in the hall lock.

"Hi . . . you're back in good time. I was about to submerge in a hot bath." She hesitated as she caught sight of the other girl's drawn features. "Hey, what's the matter with you?"

Diana shook her head slightly and put her

bag on the bureau before collapsing in a chair. She had debated telling Jill about Carlo and then decided against it. "Nothing really. Probably I just walked too far. Would you like some coffee if I call room service?"

"Always," Jill assured her. "I'm a thoughtless toad . . . dragging you all over town shopping. Why didn't you say you were tired?"

"Forget it," Diana said lightly. "I'll be as good as new after I rest for a few minutes and have something hot to drink. Did you find anything at the tack shop?"

Jill shook her head. "No, their selection is limited now, but they plan to get more stock next month so I'll go back then." She gave a cursory glance around. "You didn't buy anything, either? Weren't there any goodies down Pender Street to interest you?"

"It was certainly interesting," Diana said with veiled irony, "all sorts of surprising things."

"I'm glad you had fun."

"Umm." She stretched gracefully in her chair like a lazy cat. "I'd better order the coffee or I'll fall asleep sitting here."

"If you call them now, I'll zip through my bath and have a cup afterwards," Jill said.

"Fair enough."

The bathroom door closed behind her and Diana walked over to the telephone to call in the room service order. Then she pushed the bedspread aside, shrugged off her shoes and relaxed in a sitting position. She yawned once and pulled the pillows into a more comfortable backrest. It seemed too much trouble to even turn on the radio. Just then, the phone rang sharply.

She gave a quick look at the closed bathroom door and reached over to pick up the receiver. If the call were for Jill, she'd take the number and let her return the call when she got out of the tub.

"Hello."

"Hello . . . Jill?"

Matt's abrupt masculine tone brought Diana's heartbeat up alarmingly. Damn the man, she thought despairingly. I only have to hear his voice and I melt like snow in the sun. Well, he needn't know he had that effect.

"No . . . Dr. Reynolds," her voice was edged with formality. "It's Diana Burke. Jill's in the bath, but if you'll hang on a minute I'll call her."

"Don't bother," he cut in, equally terse, "you'll do as well. I just wanted to find what your plans were for the evening."

So now he was taking a long distance interest in guiding their social life. Diana felt a surge of unreasoning anger sweep over her. The man could run out on people, leave nasty notes, wield a heavy hand in his family life, and still expect instant compliance.

"Are you still there, Miss Burke?"

"Of course. Jill mentioned that you asked her

to help entertain Jim Dodge so we've made plans for dinner and the evening."

"Good! I'm glad she followed through." His tone became lighter with apparent relief. "Sorry about the threesome arrangement. Perhaps Jill can call one of her Vancouver acquaintances to round out your numbers."

To hear Matthew Reynolds calmly deciding she needed a blind date infuriated Diana anew.

"That won't be necessary," she said sweetly. "We already have a foursome."

"Oh?"

"Uh-huh." Her tone held deliberate malice. "You remember Carlo . . . Carlo Mangini?"

"Very well." The words sounded as if they were bit off. "So he came along with you? Jill must invite him down to Killara." He might have been asking her to pass the salt for all the interest in his voice.

"I think she plans to."

"That should be nice . . . for all of you." Again there was the dispassionate innuendo. "Tell Jill I called, will you? I'll see you later on."

"Will you be at home tomorrow?" Diana let the question slip despite her best intentions.

"I suppose so. Was there something special you wanted?"

"No . . . not really." She was flustered by then. "I thought you'd want to give me some new orders on the copying; I was fairly well caught up when I left."

He dismissed the idea summarily. "You won't want to bother with that when you have a guest. Don't worry about the notes. I'll make other arrangements."

"I see." The promising glow that had enveloped her at the beginning of the conversation faded with his impersonal words. Apparently he could turn off his interest in a woman at will. What a pity it wasn't as easy for her.

"In that case," she went on slowly, "there's no need for me to stay on at Killara."

"Don't be a little fool!" Matt's angry response indicated that she wasn't the only one having trouble maintaining her aplomb. "I don't intend to discuss that now . . . I'll see you tomorrow." There was the loud click of a receiver and then a sudden buzzing in her ear as the connection was severed.

She was still sitting bolt upright with the receiver in her hand when Jill came back into the room.

"You look like a copy of The Thinker," the blond girl said, going over to the closet. "Was it an interesting phone call?"

Diana stared at her with a puzzled expression and then her forehead smoothed out. "Oh yes, of course. It was your brother."

Jill gave her an amused look as she came back carrying a dress on a hanger. "Hadn't you better hang up the receiver?"

"The what?" Diana's glance turned sheepish as it fell upon the object still clutched in her hand. "I didn't realize . . ." The words trailed off.

"What on earth did Matt say to put the double whammy on you?"

"Nothing. He sent his best to you."

Jill hovered in the bathroom doorway. "Well, that shouldn't have a soporific effect on you. Was that all?"

"He wanted to know what we were doing this evening and seemed relieved when we were going out with Jim."

"I don't understand the sudden interest in our goings-on. Matt usually stays miles away from such involvements."

Feminine curiosity got the better of Diana. "Hasn't he been attracted to anyone in the past?"

Jill gave a sudden spurt of laughter. "Heavens yes, he's had his moments." She shifted the hanger in her hand and selected a new pair of stockings from her open suitcase. "I must say he's been discreet about showing interest in any special woman. Though, to be honest, perhaps there was less interest than discretion."

The door buzzer sounded abruptly.

"That will be our coffee," Diana said, getting up and going to open the door.

Jill headed purposefully for the bathroom. "I'll get dressed. Back in a few minutes."

Diana directed the room service waiter to put the tray on the bureau. Once the man had been tipped and dismissed, she poured a cup of coffee and took it back to the bedside table. She resumed her perch on the bed and drank thoughtfully.

Jill's words on Matt's habits hadn't come as a surprise; his behavior with her revealed full well that he wasn't an inexperienced beginner when it came to handling women. However, it was nice to know that there wasn't any thwarted love affair in his past. If she was to be sent away with a mere memory, at least it could be one she needn't be ashamed of.

Jill wafted back into the room, looking delectable in a green silk dress with a cowl collar. "The bath's all yours." She glanced at her watch. "You'd better hurry if we're to be ready on time. Can you manage in thirty minutes?"

"Easily. Have some coffee before it gets cold."

"All right." Jill helped herself and sat down in the chair by the window. "It feels good to get dressed up." She took a cautious sip. "I'm looking forward to this evening; it should be fun if Jim will only cooperate."

Diana paused en route to the bathroom. "What on earth do you mean?"

"Nothing vital. Jim can be a little hard to get along with if he has to share the spotlight with another man. He undoubtedly would have preferred a threesome."

"That was the impression your brother gave, too." Diana's lips quirked. "Poor Carlo, he does find himself in the doghouse."

"Not with me," Jill said emphatically. "I'm delighted he's coming along. Frankly, I'm tired of hearing about Jim's symptoms. Deliver me from the strong, rugged type of man if they've been near a doctor in the last six months."

"I know what you mean. Shouldn't you call Jim and warn him that we're going to have another body? It might smooth the atmosphere if they don't have to meet in the lobby."

"That's a good idea." Jill glanced at her watch again. "Jim might still be in his hotel . . . it's not far from here. I'll give him a ring."

Diana went in to run her bath water and then started tucking her hair under a bouffant shower cap. She heard Jill's tap on the door and pulled it open to see the other girl's puzzled face.

"What's the matter, couldn't you reach him?"

Jill shook her head. "I certainly couldn't."

"He's probably on his way," Diana said soothingly. "Well, it won't matter. Carlo's awfully easy to get along with. He can discuss horses with Jim all evening if they can't agree on anything else."

"It isn't that," Jill cut in. "I'm just puzzled. Jim wasn't even registered at the hotel; he'd checked out two days ago. Why on earth should he bother to lie to me?"

"I can't imagine . . ."

"Do you think I should ask him this evening?"

Diana thought of Matt's puzzling behavior, of Carlo's strange appearance that afternoon. Jim's change of hotels seemed mild in contrast.

"No," she said hesitantly. "And I wouldn't tell him you called either. Something strange is going on. Let's wait a bit and see what happens."

"All right," Jill picked up her coffee cup again. "Old do-nothing, see-nothing—that's me. I'll practice being your faithful follower."

"Follower!" Diana snorted inelegantly. "As a detective, I'm a heck of a lot more apt to need someone to pick me up when I fall flat on my face."

Chapter Eight

Diana was no nearer the truth, whatever it was, as they approached Killara in the early afternoon of the next day.

The only thing the evening had proved was that one before-dinner champagne cocktail could not be successfully mixed with one glass of Uncle Bruno's homemade wine despite Italian opinion to the contrary. The fact that Carlo was, at that moment, sitting bright-eyed and in excellent health on the back seat of the car and that she was on the front seat wishing her head would stop throbbing in time with the windshield wipers proved merely that men were definitely more hardheaded than women. It was a truism which she had suspected all along. The word boneheaded, she decided bitterly, should be substituted for hardheaded.

Carlo interrupted his deep discussion with Jill on the humane training of Tennessee walking horses to lean forward and touch her shoulder gently.

"Feeling better, *carina*?" he asked kindly.

"You won't have to call in the Doctors Mayo," she said repressively. "But never,never again will I let you talk me into anything."

He raised his hand solemnly. "I swear it is not possible to get a headache from the amount of liquor you consumed."

"Then I have just achieved a minor medical miracle."

Jill giggled. "Poor Di. What rotten luck to end up with a hangover after being cold sober all evening."

"I remember now," Carlo said solemnly. "That was one of Diana's greatest attractions . . . she was such an inexpensive date. I only had to buy her one drink each evening."

"I caught on fast," Diana said with a rueful smile over her shoulder, "after I found that the Manginis served all liquid refreshment in water goblets." She settled carefully back in the seat and looked over at Jim Dodge who was driving. "At least you didn't suffer from the wine. I wasn't sure that your doctor would approve such goings-on."

He gave her a quick, sideways glance along with a grin. "It all depends on selecting the right doctor. The only ill effects I collected from the evening are some strained back muscles. They came from trying the bugaloo with Jill. I'm getting too old for that."

Jill shook her head sorrowfully. "We'll have to put you and Diana both out to pasture. I could have danced hours longer!" She put an impulsive hand on Carlo's sleeve. "Don't forget, you promised to show me that new tango step. We'll dig out some records tonight."

"I won't forget. That is, if your brother doesn't object."

"Of course not. Say Di, we must decide on the curtains for the upper hall some time this weekend. I should let the shop in Vancouver know whether or not to go ahead."

"You'd better compare their fabric with some samples I brought with me," Diana told her. "I'll get the swatch book out of the car trunk when we get back to Killara. There's an extra set of keys in the glove compartment, so if you're down by the garage first, rummage around and select whichever you want."

"Good. I'm a little dubious about the color of that Canadian fabric." Jill looked out the window. "We're almost home . . . you can see the house now, Carlo. And there's Matt's car in the drive. I wasn't sure he'd be here."

"Why wouldn't he be?" Jim asked.

"No reason," Jill was vagueness itself. "Except that he seems so restless these days. I told him I thought he should be going to the doctor for a checkup instead of you."

"Oh-oh. What did he say to that?"

"Brrr." She shivered and ran her fingers across her throat in graphic fashion. "I'll know better than to make any more helpful suggestions in the future." She gathered up her purse and gloves as Jim turned into the Killara entrance.

"Let's hope that Mavis and Mrs. Lee have everything under control in the house."

"Now you'll see the efficient Miss Reynolds," Diana told Carlo. "That social butterfly flitting around Vancouver . . ."

". . . turns into a hard-working moth," Jill finished for her. "Or is that the way it works? Entomology was never my strong subject."

"Entomology?" Carlo gave the word an Italian pronunciation.

"The study of insects," she told him and then noticed the humorous lines around his mouth. "As you well know," she added severely. "It isn't right that a foreigner should speak English so well."

Carlo shrugged. "It's easy when you study abroad."

"And practice all your homework on beautiful English girls," Jill put in shrewdly.

Diana gave them both an amused glance over her shoulder as the car slowed to a stop. "You two should have a lively weekend." She opened her car door. "Thanks so much for acting as chauffeur, Jim."

"The pleasure's been all mine. I'll get the bags in a few minutes."

"Let me help," Carlo offered.

"No, thanks," the big foreman said casually. "They're no trouble. Right now, I'd better get down and check on a few things with Jake. I'll drop the stuff off later."

"That will be fine," Jill said absently.

"Thanks again. Don't try to do too much, too fast. You're a semi-invalid, don't forget."

"I'm feeling fine, but thanks anyway." He gave them a casual salute and drove off down the drive toward his cottage.

"Come on, you two," Jill said. "Let's go in and say hello to Matt and then I'll show Carlo the horses."

"I'm flattered that my sister lists me before the livestock." Matt spoke from the doorway behind them. He held out his hand to Carlo courteously. "It's nice to have you with us, Mr. Mangini."

Carlo gave a perfunctory bow as they shook hands. "It's kind of you to invite me. I have been looking forward to it ever since Diana told me about your home."

"I didn't know she was so enthusiastic about it," Matt said evenly. "How are you, Diana?"

"Very well, thank you, Dr. Reynolds," she said through stiff lips. The bleak tone of his voice made it all too evident that his greeting was strictly a formality.

"Are you still calling him Dr. Reynolds?" Jill asked in amazement. "Heavens, I thought you had gotten past that stage ages ago."

"I thought so too," her brother said and changed the subject abruptly. "Are you going to show Mr. Mangini to his room?"

"Make it Carlo, please," he corrected.

"Very well, Carlo." Matt smiled briefly. "Anyhow, you'd better locate your room now so you'll know where to escape when my sister plans some of her more tiring outings. Any number of house guests have had to be carted off in an ambulance after a few days."

"Pay no attention to him, Carlo," Jill said blithely. "He's just jealous because he can't keep up with me." She cast a quelling glance at her brother. "Is Diana's room ready?"

"Of course."

"Then we'll go on up." Jill ushered them through the big, open doorway. "She'd probably like to rest for a while and get rid of her headache."

"Aren't you feeling well?" Matt casually rounded on Diana at the bottom of the stairs.

"I should have known better than to try the wine," she said lightly.

"Imagine having a hangover . . ." Jill put in sympathetically only to have Matt interrupt her.

"Yes imagine," he said tersely. "Too bad, Diana. You should learn to do things in moderation. Don't bother to come downstairs until you're feeling better . . . I'm sure Jill can find some aspirin for you. And now, if you'll excuse me, I have to get back to work." He turned on his heel and disappeared in the direction of his study.

"Well, for heaven's sake!" Jill said in an injured tone. "I was just going to say that you were the only person I'd ever known to feel miserable on one glass of champagne and a sampling of wine. What rotten luck!"

Diana put her hand on the stair railing and bit her lip to keep it from trembling. "Why bother," she said brightly, "explanations are tiresome. Lead me to the aspirin and consider the matter closed."

It wasn't until later when she was lying in the quiet, darkened bedroom that she let herself face the facts squarely. There was no point in staying around merely to provide Matthew with a handy whipping post. Obviously, he had hoped to end their friendship in London. In view of his most recent remarks, there was no longer any doubt of it. Very well, she could opt out as well. Tomorrow, she would put in a call for David Royle and tell him her assignment was over. He could find his own explanation for soothing Matt's Aunt Violet. And the next time they wanted to send her on a wild goose chase like this, she'd hand in her resignation.

At that point, she gave up and turned her head into the pillow to weep like a disappointed child. Rational argument and unrequited love were poor bedfellows.

A soft knocking on her door woke her from a troubled doze some time later.

She started to answer and then clamped her lips shut. The thought of making pleasant conversation with anyone was beyond her just then. She heard the knob turn and saw the door open slightly. Deliberately she closed her eyes and lay quietly, feigning sleep.

The door closed again. She let out a sigh of relief and rose up on an elbow to turn on the lamp at her bedside. Its light revealed a tall figure standing quietly just inside the door.

"I'm sorry." Matt came slowly over to the bed. "I didn't mean to wake you. Jim just brought your bags up to the house and I thought you might need something in them."

The fact that he was there, really there, and staring down at her percolated through her sleep-dazed mind.

She ran a hand through her tousled hair and pushed up to a sitting position. "It's all right . . . I don't mean to be so fuzzy." She clutched the taffeta-covered comforter closer to her and looked down at the white wool robe she was wearing. "Heavens, look at the wrinkles. I didn't intend to go to sleep."

Matt's searching glance took in her swollen and reddened eyelids. His expression softened. "Is your headache better?"

She waggled her neck gingerly. "Very much so, thanks. I'd be more presentable after a bath, though." She swung her feet over the edge of the bed and stood up. "So if you'll excuse me . . ."

"I want to talk to you." Matt disregarded her plea and circled the bed to stare out the window. He let the silence between them build up for a minute and then turned back to give her a hooded look. "It won't take long but I think I'm entitled to a few straight answers. Go in and

183

wash your face if you want . . ." He sat down in one of the upholstered chairs. "I'll wait for you."

"Couldn't it wait until tomorrow?"

"No, it couldn't," he said calmly. "Will it bother you if I smoke?"

She shook her head and made one more effort to evict him. "I don't think you should be in here. We could talk in your study."

"And be interrupted every three minutes," he said tersely. "There's a cold mist starting to come down outside so unless you want to court pneumonia, that's out as well. If you're afraid of entertaining me in this bedroom, you could always come to mine." He allowed himself a bleak smile. "But that would look worse, wouldn't it?"

"It certainly would!" She pulled her long robe more tightly around her and gathered up her comb and lipstick from the dressing table.

He watched her dispassionately as he shook out a cigarette from the package in his pocket and proceeded to light it. "You weren't so touchy about conventions at the hotel in London."

"That was different."

"I don't see why."

She paused by the bathroom door and said in a cutting tone, "Believe it or not, I'm thinking of your reputation as well as mine. If Jill came in . . ."

"She would think nothing of it," he finished for her. "I'd like to believe she had that much sense. But if your friend Carlo should knock on the door," he paused suggestively, "I wonder if he would be so understanding."

"My friend Carlo," she mimicked his tone bitterly, "is not about to knock on the door. He has better manners." She looked to see if her verbal assault had any effect on him and noticed only a slight tensing of his jaw muscle. Trying to score off Matt was an almost impossible task, she was discovering. "Oh, never mind. I'll be back in a minute." The bathroom door closed smartly behind her.

When she emerged, the tear stains had disappeared and a slight dusting of talc had brought her eyelids back to their normal state. Her hair was once again swirled into place and an application of coral lipstick outlined the tremulous softness of her mouth.

Matt gave her a searching glance as he rose and saw her seated in the big upholstered chair beside his. She seemed as delicate as the dew on the grass, he decided. Then the illusion of frailty vanished as he looked into the grave brown eyes staring at him with cautious appraisal.

He leaned forward to offer her a cigarette. "Sure you feel up to this?"

She waved away his offer of a match and helped herself from the table lighter by the ash tray. "Your solicitude is touching but a little belated. I'm game for practically anything short of a minor Spanish Inquisition."

"For lord's sake, Diana . . . stop acting like a maligned character from a soap opera!"

Her temper flared as violently as his. "I am not acting."

"Don't tell me you behave like this normally. When I left you in London . . ."

"Left is the operative word in your vocabulary," she interrupted. "That note of yours would have curdled anyone around the edges." Tears of frustration welled up behind her eyelids and she blinked furiously to keep them back.

"I left," he gritted out, "because I had no desire to chaperone what was obviously going to be a cozy twosome."

"You mean Carlo, I suppose?"

"I certainly do mean Carlo," he said bitterly. "It's a free country, but I'll be damned if I understand why you had to bring him along here. I'm not good at playing games, Diana, and right now I haven't time to play one even if I wanted to."

So he was jealous. Underneath the cold exterior and icy facade, he did care what happened. A small vestige of hope burgeoned in Diana's breast.

He was staring moodily at the cigarette ash he had tipped into the tray. "And he isn't worth crying about. Jill should be spanked for leading him on, but I'll get her aside and tell her to behave herself."

"Matt . . ." her soft voice interrupted his bleak monologue. "You needn't bother. Jill knows exactly what's she's doing. I told her in Vancouver that Carlo was a friend of mine . . . a very dear friend," she watched his head come up abruptly and met his intent gaze, "but that's all."

His eyes darkened into a look that made her catch her breath.

"You're sure, Diana?"

"Quite sure." Now that the tense moment had passed, she let out a hiccuping sigh of relief. "So next time, make sure who's playing before you deal yourself out of the game."

He settled back and gave her a measuring look. "There's not going to be a next time . . . now. You can tell Mr. Mangini that you're booked. I don't intend to share my . . . secretary . . . with anyone. Jill can do the honors with Carlo; I want you close by." He reached over to grind out his cigarette. "Would you rather have a tray up here tonight or come down for dinner?"

She stood beside him as he got to his feet. "Oh, I'll be down." Relief from escaping his displeasure made her lighthearted. "I have to go out and pay my respects to Carmen. I haven't seen her since I got back."

"I'll go with you." He pulled her hand up to his cheek. "Look, Di, I can't explain, but I don't want you wandering around Killara on your own. After this weekend, it will be best if you

187

and Jill find an excuse to do some more traveling."

"What is this?" She lifted a bemused face. "I've never known such a man for trying to get rid of me."

He stifled a groan. "Listen, I've told you I can't explain. Just trust me, will you? It won't be for any longer than I can help."

"I do trust you, Matt. Actually, you and Jill are the only two that I do trust."

"That sounds ominous."

"Maybe I'm searching for trouble." She told him briefly about seeing Carlo in downtown Vancouver and of Jill's disgust when she found that Jim had moved to another hotel without letting her know.

Matt shrugged off the latter news, but his forehead wrinkled at hearing the story of Carlo. "Down Pender Street, eh?" He whistled softly. "What do you know? I wouldn't have said he was the type at all."

"He isn't. Do you suppose there could be a logical explanation?"

"I don't know but I'll make you a bet that he doesn't volunteer any information." He shook her gently. "You and your boy friends! Did you have any truck with Jack the Ripper?"

"No," she said consideringly, "although I once had a blind date with a college freshman who would have made Jack seem tame."

"And he went on to become a college professor."

"As a matter of fact, I think he eventually did get a master's degree in education."

"I refuse to be drawn any deeper into this discussion," he said firmly, "or I'll find myself defending the idiot and you'll end up throwing things at me."

"I did not throw anything at you."

"That bathroom door was a lot looser on the hinges after you went through it. If it happens again, I'll start docking your salary for wear and tear on the premises."

She gave him a cheeky grin. "I won't have to throw things if you've decided I'm not part of the lend-lease for needy Europeans."

"Just keep it up, young lady," he warned with his hand tightening on her shoulder.

"And?"

He looked around ruefully and dropped his hand back to his side with reluctance. "I'd better remember that you're a guest in my house, so don't tempt me, madam." Deliberately, he walked over to the window to peer through the curtains at the gathering mist. "I hope Jill and Carlo didn't wander very far in this."

"Mat, do you think there could be any connection between Carlo and that murdered man?"

He turned to face her. "Other than the fact that they're both Italians, I don't know what it would be. You've lived with the Mangini family. Was there anything suspicious about their activities or their income?"

"I'm sure there wasn't. It's a matter of record that Carlo's brother is high up in something to do with national security." Her forehead wrinkled as she concentrated. "A commission that works in liaison with the World Health people and a United Nations force." She hesitated and then looked over at Matt, excitement mounting in her expression. "Do you suppose there could be a connection?"

"I don't know," he admitted frankly. "It rather looks as if we're scraping the bottom of the barrel. Did you tell Carlo about the trouble here?"

"I can't remember." She bit her lip as she thought back. "To be honest, I probably did tell him some of it. Don't forget though, he planned to come to Vancouver before he met me at the hotel. He told us that at dinner."

"Umm." He shoved his hands into the pockets of his slacks and stared at the floor. "If he wanted to visit Vancouver so badly, then what's he doing down here after only an overnight stay in Canada?" He gave her a considering look. "The obvious answer would be that he wanted to be with you."

She moved over beside him and put a placating hand on his arm. "Now listen, let's not get back to that. I give you my word that Carlo is not in the throes of a heartbreaking love affair. We went through all this when I was staying with them. Since I've been home, I've had exactly two letters from him. Three paragraphs of the last letter were taken up with a new chestnut colt they had on their estate. You could scarcely call that the love letter of the century."

"Poor Diana." He grinned briefly. "First horses, then parasites. We'll have to do something about that later on. Well, if it's not you he's following . . . it could be Jill. What do you think of that angle?"

She shook her head slowly. "Not much. Not yet, anyway. They had a fine time dancing together and she could hardly wait to show him her horses, but other than that . . ."

"No unrequited love?"

"I don't think so. Heavens," she said defensively, "they only met yesterday."

"Does that make a difference?" His gaze was intent.

She returned it honestly. "No. Time has nothing to do with it."

There was just the trace of a smile on his face, but it was reflected in his eyes. "So we find ourselves with something else in common, Miss Burke. Remember . . . you were the young woman who was worried because you couldn't develop a passion for liver flukes."

An elusive dimple appeared at the corner of her mouth. "I'm even working on that! Well, does Carlo stay on sufferance then?"

"Of course. We've probably got the man all wrong. Maybe he's writing a book and went down to that tavern for atmosphere."

"With that background and all that was going on," she commented wryly, "it will undoubtedly hit the bestseller lists. One of those paperbacks with a cover that makes you blush."

"And when you smuggle it home, you find that the cover illustration has nothing to do with the story." He grinned. "I'd better get out of here and let you get dressed. Then we'll go down and pay a short call on Carmen."

She gave a perfunctory glance toward the window. "In this mist?"

"Sure—you won't melt. Carmen has built-in direction finders; she can hone in on a bunch of carrots from a hundred yards."

"All right. We can tell her all about her cousins in the palace guard."

There was a brief knock and the door was opened just far enough for Jill to stick her head around it. "Diana . . . how are you feeling . . . oh!" Her solicitous gaze had moved from the bed to focus on them standing together by the window. "For heaven's sake, Matt, what are you doing in here?"

Even though Diana did her best to swallow a giggle, Matt observed her efforts and turned brick red under his sister's indignant look.

"Hoping you wouldn't ask a stupid question like that," he answered bitterly.

Jill swung the door wide open but remained in the doorway. "I can imagine the questions

I'd get if you found me entertaining Carlo in my bedroom."

"Touché," Diana muttered softly for Matt's ears.

"There is absolutely no basis for comparison," he told his sister in glacial tones, "and you'd better not experiment to find out!"

"You see," Jill appealed to Diana, "another case of 'do as I say and not as I do.'"

"Jill, I forbid you to say one more word . . ."

"It's all right, Matt," Diana soothed him. "Actually, Jill, he came to bring my bags and then stayed to read me the riot act."

"Beyond that, it's none of your business, my dear sister. Where's your friend Carlo?"

"Around." Jill shrugged casually, still annoyed with him. "We looked at the horses for a while and then Jake was going to tour him around the outbuildings while I came in to see about dinner. Carlo promised to be back in good time."

"I see." Matt's look was hard to fathom as he moved purposefully toward the door. "I've a few things to attend to." He paused beside Jill and glanced back over his shoulder at the girl standing by the window. "I'll meet you down by the Carrot Queen in about a half hour. Okay?" He waited just long enough to note her shining eyes and hesitant nod before he disappeared into the hallway.

"Now what's all that in aid of?" Jill asked after she had watched him out of sight.

"Did you ever know Matt to explain?" Diana said evasively.

"Ah-hah . . . so now it's back to Matt!" Jill was triumphant. "Things are moving along from the Dr. Reynolds stage." Her pert face creased with mischief. "What I want to know is how fast they're moving along. Tell me, Di . . . what was my august brother really doing in here?"

Diana held up her hand solemnly. "Scout's honor . . . he was reading me the riot act for the first installment and deciding to let me stay around in the second . . . despite my Italian friend."

"Could I make a guess at the conclusion?"

"Don't you dare," Diana said in mock ferocity. "I've had enough trouble. No more shortcuts; everything now goes by the book."

"But where are you in the darned book?" Jill asked in frustration.

Diana drifted toward her bathroom with a dreamy smile. "In the part that says 'to be continued in the next installment.'"

From the sound of the hall door slamming behind Jill, there were going to be more loose hinges for Jake to fix the next day.

Chapter Nine

According to all signs and portents, events should then have moved along smoothly. They should have; but they didn't.

For one thing, the wrong man showed up at the rendezvous.

Diana had followed the schedule as best she could. She had bathed and dressed in a well-fitting white knit slack outfit topped with a royal blue double-breasted jacket and perky silk scarf.

There was the necessary detour past the kitchen to renew her acquaintance with Mavis, Mrs. Lee, and the crisper section of the refrigerator. Mrs. Lee merely raised her eyebrows in resignation when she saw a handful of scrubbed carrots being packed away in a plastic bag.

"Beats me what you see in that danged burro," she told Diana. "Doctor Matt was through here a little while ago checking on that carrot supply. It's a good thing I hadn't planned to have them grated for salad. As it is,

I'm supposed to tell Jake to get some more when he drives in for shopping tomorrow. Miss Jill's been bad enough with those horses of hers, but now . . ." She walked back to the stove still shaking her head, leaving Diana to escape thankfully before she received another lecture.

So Matt was ensuring Carmen's tidbits as well. She smiled happily as she made her way carefully down the path through the mist which was socking in for the night. Looking up to see how thick it was, she was surprised to note it was well on its way toward a real pea-souper fog. Both Matt and Jill had mentioned earlier that freak winds sometimes caused Killara to be isolated in the mist for a day or two at a time.

"We wouldn't have to sit home if we were closer to a main highway," Jill had said. "All you need is a center line to follow in driving and plenty of patience. There's a line on the hard surface part of our road but then you get to the gravel, and blooey." She had made an expressive gesture. "I've even known Jim to lose his way and have to sit on the shoulder of the road until the fog lifted."

"You make it sound like London," Diana had said.

"I don't know about their fogs," Jill countered, "but ours don't take a back seat to anybody. The Seattle-Tacoma air terminal has the dubious distinction of being fogbound more than any other international terminus in the whole country."

"So you just sit around and wait," Diana was amazed. "It's like the old stories of being snowbound."

"Not quite so bad because when the weather changes, we're back to sunshine in a matter of minutes. Anyhow, it's only the country places that are immobilized. The city streets and freeways all have sodium vapor lamps." Jill had made a thoughtful grimace. "You know, the funny part is . . . you get to like it. Fog stops everything at Killara and the quiet is wonderful. Like a silver shroud that covers and protects you." She laughed self-consciously. "Don't tell Jim or Jake I said so; the men don't like it at all."

As Diana stood by the split-rail fence, she felt that Jill had a good point. The peace that came with the mist was soothing to the soul. Conversely, there was an eerie disquiet when strange shapes loomed up in that same mist. The mountain ash tree standing by the fence became a fanciful thing in the murk. And even the stubby blob that was Carmen had caused a moment of alarm before Diana heard her queer, snuffly breathing and recognized her shambling gait.

There was certainly nothing supernatural about her now as she stood noisily crunching a crisp carrot and suffering her rough muzzle to be caressed.

"Didn't anyone ever tell you to chew with your mouth closed?" Diana chided her. "Your table manners are abominable, old girl. No wonder you're destined for a lonely spinsterhood."

"Is that what's her trouble?" It was an amused masculine voice behind her.

Diana whirled and let out a gasp of alarm which turned into relief as she saw Carlo watching her with amusement. "You!" She swallowed nervously. "Good heavens, you didn't have to scare me almost out of my skin. Couldn't you have shouted *Ciao* or something to warn me."

He moved up beside her and dropped a comforting arm around her shoulders. "I'm sorry, *carissima*. I was so intent upon the feeding time that I forgot about this mist." He cast a casual glance around. "You wouldn't think it would be like this in the summer."

"We're pretty far north, don't forget."

"I'm not forgetting." He pulled his coat collar up on the back of his neck. "Just for a minute, I was wishing we were in sunny Italy."

"Don't be patronizing, Signor Mangini," she scolded. "I can remember some cold winds in Trieste."

"*Si*." For the moment, he was completely European. "I think there's something about fog that makes us all a little sad and a little homesick."

She nodded. "At least, it makes us stop and

198

think. Carmen, stop that!" She removed her arm from the reach of the burro's nose. "I'm not a scratching post, you silly thing. Just a minute and I'll get you another carrot." She reached down to the plastic bag by her feet. "There you are. Gently now . . ." she warned, "and make it last a little longer. At this rate, you'll be through the summer's supply before the week is out."

Carlo watched the digestive process with amusement. "Her consumption is enthusiastic, that one."

"It certainly is. She'll never suffer from night blindness. Carrots are supposed to supply vitamin A by the bushel."

"And curly hair? Will she get that, as well?"

Diana looked dubiously at Carmen's molting nose. "She should settle for more hair of any kind. Poor thing, getting old can't be much fun for her, either."

"At least she has a nice pasture to do it in. Let's leave her to it and get back in the house." He shivered. "Blame it on my thin foreign blood if you must, but I'm freezing to death. This fog of yours is seeping into my bones."

"Poor Carlo," her tone was only half mocking. "You go on up to the house before you catch cold. I'll be along shortly."

"What is this fascination for feeding a burro?" He looked at her suspiciously. "I can't remember your spoiling my animals when you stayed with Mamma."

"I admire Carmen's independence and I feel sorry for her . . ."

"Or something. It's not like you to be evasive, little one."

"And it's not like you to be so curious. Were you by yourself out here?"

"Now we're getting to the truth," he said with some satisfaction. "I thought the interest was more in two-legged animals than four-legged ones." He smiled blandly at her obvious discomfort. "Si, there are other people around. Whom did you have in mind, specifically?"

"I don't know why I ever consented to come to Canada with you."

"Because of my continental charm. All Italians have it," he told her with amusement. "The books say so. Stop changing the subject."

"I haven't changed the subject. I was saying you should go in the house to avoid a cold in the head," she gazed up at him with exasperation, "but now I'm wondering why I was concerned about your health at all. Go wade in a cold stream somewhere!"

"And leave you in peace to meet someone else." He raised an eyebrow disdainfully. "All right, if I must. I wonder who it can be. Jim and his helper, the estimable Jake, were down by the stables when I left them . . ."

"And Matt?"

"Ah, now it comes out." He pounced on her verbally. "I didn't think I had any competition from Mr. Dodge. But Matt, now . . . he's a fish of a different stripe."

"You mean horse of a different color."

"Did I? No matter," he said shrugging. "So it's Matt. That is more difficult entirely. *Mama mia*, I will have to give up."

"I've never heard you use that expression before in your life," she accused. "You've been watching too many of those old Italian movies on television."

"I'm trying to give you some atmosphere. Don't forget, I have a reputation to maintain."

"Then go maintain it with Jill." She gave him an exasperated push up the path. "You're not helping things for me a bit. I take it you haven't seen Matt?"

He shook his head. "Not a glimpse. But if he told you he'd be here, then he undoubtedly will. I hope he doesn't keep you waiting so long that you end up with a cold in that hard head of yours." He made an elaborate ducking motion as she raised her hand. "All right, I go." He started strolling up the path. "I will have the hot toddy ready, *carina. Arrivederci*."

"*Ciao*, Carlo."

She turned back to Carmen and gave her nose another absent-minded scratch. Where could Matt be? A quick glance at her watch confirmed that he was more than slightly tardy; he just wasn't going to come. She gave an involuntary shiver as the dampness seemed to close around her ankles. Even Matt wouldn't expect her to stand here for the rest of the night.

She pulled one of the burro's long ears affectionately and looked directly into the unblinking stare. "Carmen, tell him I couldn't wait any longer, will you? I'll see you tomorrow."

After she had taken a step or two up the path toward the house, she hesitated. This would be a good time to check on her car and to get the curtain swatch book from the trunk. She turned down the walk that curved along the pasture fence toward the outbuildings, stepping carefully in the mist. The only sound was the crunching of fine gravel underneath her feet. It was entirely too desolate for comfort, she decided.

The thin beam of the spotlight on the nearest corner of the garage became suddenly as welcome as a lighthouse beam in tricky waters. She hastened her steps and turned up the collar of her lightweight jacket to keep the cold air off the back of her neck. The silk scarf had long since become more of a soggy necktie than a fashion accessory and she could feel the ends of her hair turn into clinging tendrils around her face. So much for any hope of salvaging a decent hairdo for the rest of the evening. And so much for looking glamorous on the one really important night of her life. Matt had already seen her looking like a pink-eyed rabbit after her nap; now he could feast his eyes on wet, lanky hair to boot.

She kicked a pebble in exasperation and heard it clink with a satisfying thud against the side of the building. The next time there was a rendezvous to be arranged she would pick the time and the place; one out of the fog, at least.

She pulled up short at the open garage door and felt cautiously around the corner post for a light switch. Her fingers encountered a splinter first but then made contact with the switch. The sudden illumination was almost stupefying after the murk outside and she hesitated for a moment by the door, chewing absently on her scratched thumb.

With luck, her extra set of keys should still be in the glove compartment. She went forward lightly, her soles sounding like a soft-shoe routine on the sandy concrete floor. Fortunately, the keys were in their proper place and her lips curved in a pleased smile. At least, she hadn't made the safari to the garage for nothing.

The car door closed with a thud as she made her way around to the trunk. Her key fitted smoothly in the lock and the trunk lid lifted automatically. She straightened momentarily, running an impatient hand through her damp hair to flip it back from her face. Now . . . which book was it that had the sheer curtain fabric? She bent over the thick sample cases realizing it was the first time in some days that she had thought of her profession. Strange how something that had been so important before could raise only a glimmer of interest in her mind. Even that darned subject of intestinal parasites held more fascination than nylon panels. She grinned wryly as she shifted the trunk cargo. How Matt would tease her if he knew her feelings on that!

Naturally, the case she wanted was at the bottom of the pile, and as she heaved it up, a small packet fell out of the cover onto the trunk floor.

Diana wrinkled her forehead as she reached down to pick it up. Now what had she brought along by mistake? Probably one of David Royle's experiments that were often shelved in the supply room or thrown anywhere he chose to discard them.

This was a small plastic bag filled with a white substance looking much like dried milk. Its top was secured by an inch-wide cardboard band. She hoisted the bag carelessly; probably it was a new substance to check moisture on plaster walls or something similar that Royle's Interiors was testing. Darn David anyway! What in the world was she supposed to do with it? Unless it was more carefully packed, the sharp edge of a sample book would poke a hole in the bag and she'd have it all over the floor of the trunk. Probably the best thing to do would be to take it up to the house and put it in a more sturdy covering.

She tucked it under one arm and pulled out the sample book with the other, resting it against the bumper while she struggled to close the trunk lid. The next time she phoned David, she'd tell him where his precious sample had gotten to and ask him to be more careful with his playthings.

Jim Dodge loomed up in the mist just before she got to the door.

"Hi," she said gaily. "I'm glad to have some company. Would you have a free hand to turn off the light switch?"

"Sure." He gave her an intent look as he lingered beside her. "Where are you taking that stuff?"

"Up to the house. I thought I'd better come down and get the sample book I promised Jill for her curtain material."

"And the other?" He nodded toward the plastic bag dangling from her fingertips.

"This?" She held it at eye level. "It must be some whim of my boss's that got stuck in my swatches by mistake. I'll take it up and see if Jill or Matt can find something better to pack it in." She gave him a brief smile. "Are you going my way?"

He uttered an explosive sigh and put a firm hand on her wrist.

"No, Diana . . . I think you're going to have to go mine." A black, stubby-looking gun appeared effortlessly from his deep jacket pocket. "Now . . . give me that plastic bag," he said tersely.

"This! What in the world do you want with . . ."

205

Dazed, her voice trailed off as she noted the lettering on the cardboard band. "Vancouver's leading feed dealer," she read as if by rote. Her eyes widened as she saw Jim snatch away the bag and thrust it in another pocket of his jacket. "So it wasn't from New York, after all," she said in a monotone. "That belonged to you, didn't it? Should I make a guess what it is?"

He tightened his fingers cruelly on her arm and shoved her toward the driver's seat of the car. "Just shut up and get in and drive. Don't try anything, Diana." He slammed the driver's door shut behind her and moved quickly around to the passenger side to slide onto the wide seat beside her. "Now, put those keys in the ignition and get this heap out of here." He jabbed the gun savagely into her side and grinned sardonically at her gasp of pain. "That's so you'll know I mean business. Get going and don't drag your feet, lady."

Obediently, she turned the ignition key and felt the engine catch and start smoothly on the second try. She backed the car out onto the concrete apron, switching on the headlights as she did so.

"Which way?"

"Which way do you suppose?" he said roughly. "I'm sure as hell not heading for the main house. Move this car onto the road or you won't be around to enjoy the last part of the trip."

"But the fog . . ."

"Damn the fog! I'll tell you which way." He watched her swing the car around the drive and head toward the entranceway. "Keep remembering . . . it would be a lot simpler for me to drive myself."

Diana took her eyes off the track long enough to look in the rear-view mirror and see if any headlights were following them, but only thick, gray mist was reflected in the glass. Evidently they were to drive off unnoticed just as the man beside her hoped. She bit down on her lip hard as the car swerved crazily onto the soft shoulder.

"Watch it," he shouted. "Hit the dimmer switch . . . you can't drive in this stuff with your bright lights on."

She stabbed at the foot switch and noted the increased visibility with relief. At least she had a better chance of seeing the edges of the road with the low beam.

"Slow down until you pick up the main track just beyond the entrance," he told her, peering carefully through the window but keeping his gun suggestively by her side. "There it is," he said triumphantly. "Now all you have to do is keep your eye on that white center line and go."

"What happens when we get to the gravel?"

"We face that problem when we get to it. By then, we might be out of this stuff altogether. It's patchy plenty of nights up here."

"You've been out sneaking around in the

middle of the night long enough to know, haven't you?" she said, giving him a quick glance.

"Keep your eyes on the road," he commanded instantly. "And when I want a sermon I'll ask for one."

"Sorry." Her tone was grim. "I wasn't trying to reform you."

"That's good. Even my mother gave up on that a long time ago." He managed a quick look over his shoulder. "There doesn't seem to be anybody behind us, but I'd feel easier if I'd had time to cut the phone wires. There's no use in underestimating our Dr. Reynolds, so keep a heavy foot on that accelerator." He resumed his sideways stance on the seat.

"Just driving through this murk is hard enough," Diana's foot was steady on the gas pedal. "Don't ask me to go any faster. I'm going ten miles an hour faster than anybody in their right mind would do now."

"So who's in their right mind these days?" He pulled a cigarette from his pocket and put it to his lips. "Isn't that what lawyers claim? Not guilty by virtue of temporary insanity. Come on, Miss Burke," he goaded her, "we've got a little time before we hit the main road and head south. Aren't you going to beg me to throw myself on the court's mercy and see if I can't get a reduced sentence for all this?"

Diana gripped the wheel so tightly that her knuckles showed white, but her tone was carefully casual. "There isn't any use kidding you. I don't think they give reduced sentences for distributing the stuff in your plastic bag. What is it . . . heroin?"

His silence was answer enough.

"I'm the stupid one," she went on conversationally.

Somehow it was better to talk than sit in the car and hear only the sound of the tires on the wet surface of the road as they plunged through the grayness of the night.

"I didn't have the . . . should I say foggiest idea . . ." her mouth curved derisively, "that it was anything incriminating until you showed up."

He gave a bark of laughter. "Unfortunately, I couldn't count on Matt's being so naive. He's been too eager to keep me away from the ranch ever since he got back. I don't know what he was up to, but there was no point in pressing my luck. If you'd kept your nose out of the car trunk, I could have gotten this stuff on its way without anybody tumbling to it."

"I doubt that. Especially since you left that distribution man to die in the ditch."

His gun hand tensed and then relaxed again. "You almost bought it, lady . . . watch what you're saying."

The car shot forward as if giving vent to her feelings.

"Don't play cat and mouse, Jim. I can't see you letting me walk over to the nearest telephone when we get to the junction. Would it do any good to promise that you'd have a head start . . .?"

"No deal. I know your kind; if you didn't have your fingers crossed, something else would be. On the other hand, it might be good to keep you around until we get to Seattle. By then, I could think of some practical use for you . . . other than the obvious one, of course."

The oozing sarcasm of his tone made her shrink as far toward her door of the car as she could. She slowed for a banked curve in an especially thick patch of mist and then pulled her speed up again as the gun jabbed into her side.

"I wish you'd stop doing that," she said truculently. "Do you think I'm so feeble-minded that I'll forget it's there?"

He snorted but pulled the gun back a bit. "You're a nice piece of skirt, but I haven't known you long enough to really get acquainted. The other night I could see you were a lot more taken with that Carlo character than you were with me."

"Then he's not a friend of yours?"

"Mangini? Never saw him before. My God, you didn't think he was part of this racket, did you? At least, not that I knew anything about." His tone grew suspicious suddenly. "What are you trying to pull?

"Nothing, I tell you." She risked a quick glance at him and then stared straight ahead again. "I ran into him in a grim part of Vancouver and couldn't decide what he was doing there."

He laughed. "You aren't the first woman to think you've got all of a man and then find that he had other ideas. Maybe Mangini got tired of trying to be the cocked-hat gentleman that you and Jill thought he should be." His resentment surged to the surface. "Now there's another one who thinks she's the answer to all mankind."

Diana strove to change the subject. "You really had Jill confused when you checked out of your hotel early. Where were you . . . back in a nursing home?"

"A nursing home! Lady, you aren't even dry behind the ears. Did you fall for that ulcer routine?"

"I thought you were seeing a doctor."

"The doctor was a friend of mine. His qualifications got a little tarnished when he served time a while back, but he remembered enough medicine to write an alibi when I needed one. It gave me the free rein I wanted for my collections and deliveries."

"So you've been at this for some time." From her dispassionate tone, they might have been discussing a change in the weather. "Did you shut me in the cabin that day?"

"You're mighty busy with the questions. Why do you think I was to blame for that?"

"Because you wouldn't even know about it if you weren't. I'm sure Matt didn't mention it

211

after we got back. Besides," she shifted restlessly in the seat, "Matt was paying so much attention to those fresh tracks in the corral that it made me suspicious. It wasn't until later that I realized you were the only one who would have brought Carmen up there that day. I've been wondering why you took such a chance."

"You can keep right on wondering."

"Very well. On an outside chance, I'd say that you met your delivery man somewhere up there. Ever since his murder, I've been racking my brain to remember what I've read about drug trafficking across the border. They're just now talking about radar sensors to monitor air traffic in remote areas, so I doubt if they're monitoring the surface traffic as yet. Think of the freedom you had to cross that long, unfenced border through the mountains. The foreman of Killara could be back and forth all summer without anyone raising an eyebrow. Since all the firewood by the cabin was gone, it makes me think you had quite a stream of visitors. It would be a handy way to avoid immigration for some of your business partners, to say nothing of customs."

"I could do without your crackpot ideas."

"All right, I'll give up," she said wearily. "I'm just afraid if I stop talking you'll hear my teeth start chattering."

"So let's try that for a change." He peered intently through the windshield. "This hard surface road is about to run out and we'll be on

212

gravel in a minute; that means it won't be long until the main road. The fog's thinning, too, so we can get a little more speed but watch what you're doing and don't get any fancy ideas. Being slammed into a tree isn't part of my plan."

"I know that," she said grimly.

The car was quiet as they both concentrated on the road ahead.

"The fog may be thinning, but it's getting patchier, too," Diana said. "I'm afraid to try any more speed. If we hit a blind spot and there's no center line to follow, we'd be off the road in a second."

He gave a sharp look at the speedometer. "Keep it the way it is, then. I wish to God I was driving."

She was too exhausted by the strain to attempt a reply. The only thing now was to drive and hope for a miracle when they got on the main road. Surely Matt would have missed her by now and phoned an alarm. On the other hand, she reasoned desperately, people don't call the police just because someone's missing for a few minutes. Unless Matt happened to notice that her car was gone, it was far more likely that he'd be out beating the bushes by Carmen's pasture. What a pity that sturdy little burro wasn't here now to sink her strong yellow teeth into Jim Dodge. The animal had more sense than they had given her credit for!

"Watch it! Here's the change in the road,"

Jim said tensely. "Slow down till you get the feel of the loose gravel and don't try anything sudden."

"Stop giving me orders," she pleaded. "If you want to drive, I'll pull up and . . ."

The hard gun barrel was against her side instantly.

"You'll stay right where you are. I'm not taking any chances with you disappearing by the side of the road. Now, get your speed back up again easy-like. This heap of yours is so light that it would fishtail just thinkin' about it."

Cautiously Diana pressed down on the accelerator and glanced again up to the rear-view mirror. A brief glimmer of light flickered behind them and disappeared.

Her heart leaped like a wild thing and her breathing almost choked her! Dear heaven, could it be?

Deliberately she forced her attention straight ahead. Out of the corner of her eye, the trailing glimmer appeared again. She wasn't seeing things; there was someone trailing them! For the first time since she had entered the car, she made a conscious effort to discipline her chaotic thoughts. If only there were some way to stall until . . .

"Now what are you thinking about?" The man beside her gave her a suspicious look.

"Nothing." She kept her voice level with an effort. "It's too hard to drive and talk at the same time."

"It didn't bother you before." He shifted uneasily. "I think I liked it better that way."

She kept her eyes away from the telltale mirror. "There's no pleasing you. Besides, you made me do all the talking."

"That's right. I'm not admitting anything."

"Even about the man in the ditch?"

"I had a perfect alibi, remember?" There was irony in his tone. "The boys'll tell you I was up with the mustering team."

"And burros don't talk. I wonder if your alibi would be as good if they checked the times a little closer?"

"Talk all you like, lady. I'm not saying I agree with you."

She risked another quick glance at the mirror. The glimmer of light had definitely gained on them! Her foot eased slightly on the accelerator.

"I don't see why you're being so chary about it," she protested, feeling as if she were leading a double existence: one part maintaining this inane conversation and the other praying for the driver in the following car. "After all, I don't have a tape recorder along and it would just be my word against yours." A cold silence met her efforts and she glanced over to see him staring sullenly ahead. "All right. Don't admit anything. I'll imagine the worst."

"Now that does break my heart, sister."

How could she ever have thought a Western

drawl was attractive! If she lived to watch another late movie on television, she'd turn it off if there was a cowboy even on the fringes of it.

She pulled her mind back to the subject under discussion and continued as if he hadn't spoken. "Why did you leave that man to die by the roadside after you beat him up?"

"If somebody," he put emphasis on the second word, "beat him up, they probably didn't think he'd croak." Scorn was evident in his voice. "These damned foreigners—they've got no stamina!"

The thought of itinerant foreigners withering before his muscles sent hysterical laughter coursing through her and she choked it back with difficulty.

"But why was there a fight in the first place?" she asked. "Aren't the plans on an operation this big worked out well in advance? I don't know what that packet in your pocket is worth, but I should imagine that it's a great deal of money."

"Now you're getting warm." He felt his jacket pocket as if to reassure himself that the precious package was still there. "More money than I can spend in a long, long time."

"I thought so." She eased back on the accelerator a fraction more and saw the speedometer needle flicker downward again. "So why the body and the danger of having the police around?"

"Probably because the bastard tried to get greedy and change the split. The boys in charge will know better than to send a creep like that again."

"Is that what you were arranging in Vancouver?"

"All I'm saying is that when a deal's made with Jim Dodge, nobody's changing the price." There was a sudden silence following his impassioned words. "Say," he spoke abruptly, "what in the hell are you draggin' anchor for? The fog's not that bad." He gave her a suspicious look and then, made uneasy by her pallor, swerved to stare through the rear window.

Two lowered headlights were plainly discernible behind them, glowing brightly at times because of the erratic thinning of the mist as the road curved or dipped in elevation.

"So that's it!" Sudden rage filled his voice. "You're doing your best to put a noose around my neck. I told you to get going!"

Deliberately, cruelly, he crushed his heavy cowboy boot over Diana's instep on the accelerator and shoved floorward.

"Stop it," she screamed as the car spurted forward. "You'll kill us!"

"Not if you watch what you're doing." He shoved the gun hard against her. "At this point, I don't care much which way we go out, so do your best, sister."

It was at that moment she saw flashing red

lights across the road in front of them and stiffened sharply.

Dodge's reaction came just afterward, but the tardy lifting of his foot from the accelerator prevented all hope of the car's stopping in time.

As if in a living nightmare, she noted the emergency vehicle blocking their path and drainage ditches at the sides of the road forestalling any possible turning or escape. Her car hurtled down on top of the lights and she knew, hopelessly, that a sudden braking on the loose gravel would cause it to veer out of control.

From the corner of her eye, she could see Jim Dodge tense on the seat beside her claw at the door with frantic hands.

It was the thought of his possible escaping more than anything else which prompted her to slam on the brake pedal and pull at the steering wheel simultaneously. The car reacted immediately and violently, lurching sideways to thrust them both forward toward the windshield and the blinking red lights which now covered them with their deathly glow. A last sense of self-preservation made Diana's fingers struggle toward the ignition key as the grinding crash and creak of metal burst upon the night.

Sudden darkness blanketing her mind brought relief from the stinging, sharp pain—relief from the terror wrought by the man beside her.

And when the harrowing shriek of metal had finally ground to a stop, her crumpled figure was as unmoving as the tall, fog-wreathed trees standing by the roadside . . . standing aloof from the mortal destruction beneath their boughs.

Chapter Ten

Diana's fog-shrouded existence continued.

There was a passage of time where she opened her eyes to an awareness of pain, the jumbled memory of hushed voices, and then the enveloping grayness that blotted out all thought.

Time wrought its healing force until the day arrived when she opened her eyes with a new awareness, when the pain had receded and her headache dulled to almost nothing. She surveyed the plain, antiseptic-looking walls of the room around her and focused with difficulty on an anxious figure sitting by her bedside.

"Jill?" she murmured carefully, as if afraid to disturb this new-found existence.

Jill moved closer and bent over her, smiling. "Thank heavens, Di. We thought you were going to sleep the week away. About ready to stay with us for a while?" Her hand groped for the nurse's call button. "Just take it easy, dear . . . the doctor wanted to be notified as soon as you were awake."

"I thought it was a hospital," Diana's voice was gaining strength. "This room could use an interior decorator."

Jill squeezed her hand reassuringly. "No insults about the surroundings until you're out of them. Oh Di, I'm so glad you're better!"

"Talk about understatements," Diana chided. "So am I, Jill. Oh, so am I!"

From then on, her medical prognosis improved until the day, a week later, when the doctor lingered by her bed and said regretfully, "If I keep you in this place any longer, they'll be after me for malpractice."

"Then I can go home?" A becoming flush spread over her pale cheeks. "When?"

He shook his head in mock sorrow. "So that's what you think of us."

"Doctor, you know I'll always be grateful for the wonderful care . . ."

"Hold on there," he interrupted her earnest speech. "I'm kidding you, of course. If you didn't want to go home at this stage, I'd turn you over to the psychiatrist. I've told Miss Reynolds she can pick you up after lunch so you've plenty of time for the nurse to get you packed. Only a word of caution, Miss Burke . . . you had a nasty concussion along with severe shock. Just because we're letting you out of the hospital doesn't mean you're to embark on any marathons for a while. You're darned fortunate that you came through as well as you did."

"I know," she said soberly. "I heard that Jim Dodge didn't regain consciousness."

"From what I've read in the press accounts and from what I know that didn't get in the newspapers, it's probably just as well." He gave her a searching look. "Don't waste time feeling sorry for a man like that, Miss Burke. If you'd seen as many wrecks of human beings as a result of narcotic drug addiction as I have, you'd say good riddance to all the money-grubbing criminals like Jim Dodge. I hope they rounded up the whole tribe of them. They wouldn't hesitate to commit any crime in the book for the sake of lining their pockets.

"Now, get up and get dressed so you'll be ready. I've given Dr. Reynolds all my instructions as well so he'll be keeping a firm hand on you out there."

"I thought he was out of town."

"That man pops around more than a Mexican jumping bean, but he manages to get in here often enough. Just because he doesn't come during visiting hours doesn't mean he misses a thing. The first two nights you were here, we couldn't get him farther away than the hall corridor. It was a near thing and he was deeply worried. Fortunately for all of us," his dry smile emerged again, "you cooperated by getting well. Now, don't fall off one of Jill's horses at Killara and undo all my good work."

"I promise." She held up her hand solemnly.

"There's a burro about five feet tall who's just my speed right now."

"Excellent. I wish more of the people in this horsy neighborhood would follow your example. Come back and see us when you're in town." He paused at her door. "A strictly social call, of course."

Diana was waiting in the foyer after lunch when Jill drove up to the main entrance. Carlo, sitting beside her in the passenger's seat, hurried out of the car to assist the dark-haired girl onto the commodious back seat. There were two pillows and a blanket piled at one end of it.

"Hey, I refuse to be propped up like an invalid back here," Diana protested.

"Hush up, honey chile, and do as you're told," Jill said briskly. "We're merely carrying out the master's orders. Instructions are that you're not even to be joggled—let alone scratched."

"Where is Matt?"

"At the ranch and madder than two wet hens because he wasn't on the reception committee," Carlo informed her, getting back in the front beside Jill and sitting sideways on the seat so he could talk to Diana. "How do you like my slang? When I get back to Trieste, the family will not be able to understand me."

"I can't tell whether you are improving or deteriorating," Diana told him solemnly, "but I have a feeling the college professors wouldn't approve."

"One college professor approves of him, at least," Jill said smugly. "As soon as Matt found he was over here on business rather than just trailing a beautiful woman, namely you, the atmosphere lightened considerably."

Diana settled back on the pillows. "You'd better start from the beginning of things, then. It's time you let me into the world again."

Jill gave a troubled glance to Carlo, who shrugged his shoulders in return.

"Perhaps it would be as well," he said noncommittally.

"I'd like it straight, please," Diana told him. "First of all, what in the world were you doing in that awful section of Vancouver?"

He shook his head desolately. "That's what happens when I try to play detective; I go out one afternoon and get noticed by the one person I want to avoid. No wonder my brother tells me to stick to my law practice."

"You can also stick to my question."

"All right, *carina*. For the beginning of it all, we have to go back to Italy. You knew that my brother Alfonso had dealings with crime detection in our country. Actually, he is a member of an international group working to try to stop the increasing traffic in drugs which has come into our country. They work in partnership with your Bureau of Narcotics men who are assigned to Italian ports."

"I remember there was an intensive baggage search the last time I disembarked at Brindisi," Diana said. "Were the customs men searching for drugs?"

"Very probably. All of our ports are vulnerable; we are so close to the sources of supply. The Mideast countries are cooperating with the United Nations and the World Health people, but there is so much money involved that it's difficult to enforce the laws. Now, in addition, opium is coming from China to some of the communist-bloc countries for partial refining. Then it's being slipped over our borders and onto our ships for delivery in the Western world. Canadian ports, since they are open to ships from the iron curtain countries, are prime targets for this traffic."

"I can understand that," Diana nodded, "and I can get a glimmer of how you came to be involved."

"It's not difficult," he conceded. "As a main seaport for northern Italy, Trieste is under constant surveillance by the police. Lately, there has been evidence that drugs are put aboard our freighters there—in with the cargo—and later unloaded at Canadian ports.

"When the body of the man was discovered at the Killara junction, his fingerprints were immediately traced by the international authorities. It didn't take long to find that he was one of the key suspects in the Italian narcotic drug movement. The next thing my brother and his associates wanted to know was why he was in the northwestern corner of the United States."

"So your trip to Canada came about," Diana hazarded.

"Now there you are wrong, Diana. My Uncle Bruno in Vancouver has so many business interests that they are beginning to interfere with his golf game. He writes to my mamma that he would like to dispose of some of them, but he wants to make sure he takes care of all the tax . . . what do you call those holes?"

"Loopholes," supplied Jill.

"*Grazie* . . . that's it . . . the tax loopholes. But Uncle Bruno sees no point in hiring a lawyer when his nephew Carlo will be in London, which is practically next door."

"And Carlo is still in London when brother Alfonso decides he'd like the lowdown on what's going on in this part of the country."

"Exactly, my dear Jill." He beamed over at her delectable profile. "Imagine my delight, then, when Diana appears and tells me she is staying at Killara. It seemed like fate. I called Alfonso and told him. He advised me to stick like glue to Diana . . ."

"To provide an alibi for your sudden appearance," she put in dryly.

"And a pleasant one! In addition, my brother wired the proper Canadian police authorities in Vancouver for their cooperation. It was they who suggested I make the acquaintance of some Italian seamen in the Pender Street tavern. But by then, the police were also onto Mr. Dodge's trail and they welcomed the chance to put in another man at Killara without arousing his suspicions. What none of us suspected was that events would move as quickly as they did."

"I'm afraid I precipitated them," Diana said meekly. "Talk about idiots walking around . . ."

"It wasn't your fault," Jill put in stoutly. "I was nearly as much in the dark, because Matt hadn't told me anything, either."

"He was under orders not to," Carlo said patiently. "After he got back from London, the authorities told him that Jim Dodge's frequent trips over the border had attracted their attention. They looked more closely into his background then, and discovered he had served time in his early twenties for narcotics possession. They could have called him in for questioning, but they felt they would rather wait and see if they could catch him with the evidence."

"How did they know there was any evidence?"

"That was the reason for our night out in Vancouver," Jill said ironically. "I should have known Matt's concern wasn't about my social life. The police had a search warrant and went through Jim's belongings at the cottage inch by inch, but they didn't want him to suddenly appear while they were doing it."

"They didn't find the packet of dope."

"But they did, Diana," Carlo said patiently. "Dodge had it hidden in a dummy butane tank on his camper bumper. So then, all they could do was sit and wait. Any strange faces at Killara would have been suspected immediately, so Matt and Jake were going to take turns spelling each other on the watch. Naturally, when you appeared with me in tow, I was under suspicion right away. When I was finally able to get Matt alone, I convinced him that I could help on their stake-out."

"So that's what you were doing when you were out wandering around in the fog?"

He nodded. "I had just left Matt who thought he had better check on Mr. Dodge. He discovered the empty butane container on the ground by the camper and realized Jim had moved the evidence. By the time he got to the garage, you were pulling out of the drive."

"So he made a mad dash for the house," Jill took up the story, "and shouted for us to call the state patrol. Before I could even answer him, he was flying down the steps and into his car after you." Her face was sober as she glanced at Diana in the rear-view mirror. "Patrol headquarters was lucky to have a car practically at the junction on the main road. They had been out in conjunction with a search-and-rescue unit for a missing child. The child turned up later at a friend's house, thank goodness. Anyhow, the patrol car set up the roadblock, never dreaming that Jim would have you careening down the road at that speed."

"The patrolmen weren't hurt, were they?" Diana's tone was horror-stricken.

Carlo shook his head. "No, fortunately, they were out of the car and waiting at the side of the road for you to appear. Then the crash occurred, and the two of them were getting you out of the wreck as Matt drove up. One stayed at the scene to radio for assistance while the other policeman and Matt took you in to the hospital. The doctor said it was a good thing they got you there when they did."

There was a sudden silence in the car as the three of them once again remembered the tragic happenings of that night.

"I hope that it doesn't spoil Killara for you, Di," Jill ventured finally as the car emerged into the open road by the entrance.

Diana looked out at the grassy meadows— soft and inviting in the afternoon sunlight— and the gracious house standing at the end of the road.

"Killara's a dream come true," she said softly. "Nothing could spoil that for me."

Jill pulled the car up in front of the flagstone terrace.

"In that case, Di, on behalf of the Reynolds family . . . welcome home!" Jill spoke quickly to mask the emotion in her voice. "Carlo will bring your bag along and we'll all have tea."

Diana gave a gurgle of laughter. "Wasn't

there a song like that? All right, I'd love to 'take tea' with you but give me a minute to go down and see Carmen while I sniff the fresh air." She caught Jill's admonishing look. "I promise I won't stay long. All right?"

Jill capitulated before her urging. "If you promise. Matt hoped to be back by now, so I'll tell Mrs. Lee to make it tea for four."

Carlo gave a permissive smile and turned to Jill. "We might even find time for a ride down the south fork later on."

Diana slipped out of the car. She grinned briefly over her shoulder as she moved quickly and happily down the path toward the pasture where an untidy gray burro was rubbing its nose on the rail fence.

Then, out of the corner of her eye, she saw a palomino horse and rider galloping down the path by the foreman's cottage. She veered direction at the same moment Matt recognized her and turned his mount to intercept her.

They met at the corner of the stable, Matt pulling up in rodeo fashion with a cloud of dust and Diana in a dead run. Suddenly he was on the ground beside her and she was clasped by a pair of strong arms.

"Darling, let me look at you." He gently raised her head from its resting place on his wool shirt front and stared down at her.

She could have happily drowned in that look.

He gave a low groan. "What a place to

meet you! Carlo and Jill on the terrace . . . Mrs. Lee and Mavis undoubtedly peering through the kitchen windows. We'd have more privacy at a freeway intersection." His hands tightened possessively around her waist. "You know," he confessed hesitantly, "I didn't think this day would ever come. If you want to go more than shouting distance from me again, you'll have to have written permission . . . do you understand?"

"Are you putting in a claim, mister?" Her voice was uneven.

"I'm all for registering it as soon as possible." His tone brooked no possibility of defeat. "You are going to marry me, aren't you, Di?"

"Oh, Matt . . . yes! If you really want me."

"Want you!" His arms tightened around her still more. "I've wanted you so long that it seems to me I ache with it. It had better be soon . . . I can't hold out much longer."

She laughed tremulously. "At least we're in the same state. Oh, heavens," she pulled away from him hurriedly, "here comes Jake to unsaddle Bob."

"One more person is just what we need," Matt said bitterly as he pulled the reins over Bob's ears and turned him around to point toward the stable before giving him a slap on the flank. "Let's get out of here or Jill and Carlo will come down to see what's happening, as well."

"They're waiting tea for us in the house."

He took her fiercely by the elbow. "Then they'll have to wait."

"And poor Carmen's waiting up there by the fence. Come on, Matt," she gave him a warm smile, "just for a minute."

"You should be resting . . ."

"Now don't you start that." Her look was entreating. "The doctor says I'm fine, so there's no need for you to wrap me in cotton wool."

"Is it all right if I cherish you just a little bit?" he asked humorously but with an earnest undertone. "I've never had anything so nice belong to me before."

She stopped abruptly in the middle of the path. "Don't say things like that, Matt, or I'll break down right here and cry."

"In front of Carmen!" he exclaimed in mock horror. "You wouldn't dare!" He walked her along at a furious pace toward the fence. "Very well, I'll revert to my normal, obnoxious self . . . as Jill would say. Promise that you won't encourage any more Italian admirers now that you've been spoken for."

"I promise," she said demurely, "but you must admit that Carlo is a dear."

"Jill would probably be the first to agree with you," he said ruefully. "She's already planning to take a vacation abroad and stay with the Manginis."

"Wonderful! She'll be a sensation in Italy with that lovely blond hair."

"Time will tell," he grinned, "but let's not

linger on the subject of trips abroad. I still get a sharp twinge of conscience when I think of my bleak departure from London."

"So you should," she said severely. "The only way we can exorcise that memory is to go back again and have you behave properly."

"Which means that on our next trip if any of your former continental acquaintances appear to talk over old times, I'll punch them in the nose, sling you over my shoulder, and head for our hotel room. That's what I wanted to do when Carlo came on the scene."

Her cheeks flushed. "Did you feel like that, too? I thought I was the only one."

"Darling . . ." He started to pull her toward him and then looked around in frustration. "Damn this goldfish bowl!"

"Never mind." She moved up to Carmen, who was waiting impatiently by the fence. "I'm sorry I don't have any carrots, old girl."

"Don't feel sorry for her. She's consumed bushels of them lately. I'm also very much aware that you're changing the subject."

"I'd better, hadn't I," she looked up at him mischievously, "considering our surroundings?"

His eyes seemed to darken as he looked at her.

She dropped her head in confusion. "Tell me," she said, striving to regain a vestige of composure, "why did you send me to London? Those slides weren't that important, were they?"

He shrugged. "Who's to say what's important?"

"Now who's changing the subject!"

"All right, maybe they weren't," he conceded, grinning. "There were two reasons. The main one was I didn't like the thought of your being alone here when Jill was in Vancouver. That escapade at the cabin appeared more than a prank when one added a murdered man to the muddle. I thought something strange was going on at Killara and I didn't want you around."

"Then you were wondering what Carmen's hoofprints were doing in that corral, too?"

He nodded. "I certainly was. She hasn't been used for any pack work officially since her hoof got so bad. It was easy to jump to conclusions, but not fair to the people around here. By the time I got back, the authorities had drawn a line on Jim from his past record."

"So Carlo was telling me." She looked down at the ground. "Let's not go over that again." Hesitantly, she asked, "What was the second reason?"

"The second reason?"

"Stop teasing. One reason you wanted me in London was because you were worried . . . but what was the second?"

"I tried to rationalize all sorts of reasons when I was sitting in England," he said quietly. "Eventually I worked out the truth: I was only functioning at half speed when you weren't around. I found myself wanting to hear your voice, looking for a glimpse of that glossy chestnut hair and your lovely smile. Getting through those interminable meetings in the daytime was bad enough, but the nights were pure hell." He held her hand against his cheek. "I think you must be part witch; you started working your spell that night at Trail Creek cabin, and I haven't been the same since."

She laughed softly. "Don't think you're the only one. I didn't know a platonic overnight stay could be so shattering."

"How would you like to go back there for a honeymoon?"

"Could we?" Her face glowed. "Oh, Matt darling, that would be wonderful! This time I'll take all the right things so you won't have to make allowances for such a greenhorn."

"I like greenhorns," he maintained stoutly. "In a week or two, Jake'll have the place cleaned up and can install a few of the amenities. By then, you'll be feeling up to par and the wedding guests will have had time to arrive." He smiled down at her in a way that made her bones melt. "We'll invite Aunt Vi so I can thank her properly for my birthday present. Speaking of presents, your get-well clock was air-freighted from London today. Each time it chimes the quarter hour, it can remind you that I was counting the minutes until we were together again. Stop crying, beautiful, or you'll have to dry your eyes on my shirt because I forgot a

235

handkerchief. Besides, you distract me."

She rubbed her head against his shoulder. "That works both ways, darling."

He stared at her, bemused. "See what I mean? Where was I? Oh, yes ... the wedding guests. You'd better invite your boss, he's been burning up the telephone wires while you were in the hospital."

She managed a watery smile. "I'll tell him the assignment will be taking longer than I planned ..."

"By about thirty or forty years. I'll find all sorts of projects for you ... you can decorate the cabin first ..."

"And then the stable ..."

"And then the nursery." He grinned at her confusion. "There'll be pictures of Carmen on the walls ..."

"Plus your fascinating discourses on the liver fluke in the bookcase."

He gave a shout of laughter. "Darling, you've got that subject on the mind."

"Darling," she mimicked, "I've got you on my mind and if you don't kiss me pretty soon, I won't have a mind left."

"Hush," his mouth was softly caressing her closed eyes and cheeks. "You talk too much."

"That's all I've had a chance to do so far," she murmured happily. "I thought I was going to have to throw myself into your arms again this time. Carmen doesn't provide much help without a carrot."

"My adorable Diana," he raised his head to look down on her in tolerant exasperation, "this is not the time to be discussing the vegetable crop."

"So stop me, Dr. Reynolds . . ."

And Dr. Reynolds did, with a kiss that drove every coherent thought from both their minds and silenced all attempts at further conversation.

They didn't get back to the subject of vegetables in season until two weeks later.

In the meantime, there had been a beautiful wedding service in the tiny mountain chapel and a sparkling reception at Killara afterward. Guests ranged from a university president to a neighboring sheep-herder. Matt's Aunt Vi took credit for the entire romance while dividing her time between David Royle and Carlo.

Diana left her beautiful lace wedding dress in the closet of the master bedroom and changed into jeans and a striped shirt for her going-away outfit to the cabin.

Conversation during their ride up the trail had been desultory, both of them finding it difficult to speak rationally when their hearts were behaving in a very irrational manner. Diana tried to come back to earth for a few minutes with mention of their grocery list.

"I hope I thought of everything we'd need," she told Matt seriously as they rode side by side. "Jill helped me make it out because she's still better at things like that. We should have enough to feed an army. Do you suppose Jake managed to transport it without too much trouble?"

"He was doing fine the last time I saw him," Matt said. "Besides, Jake's not one to fuss. Looks as if we've arrived."

As they rode into the clearing, the hoofprints of Jake's horses were clearly visible in the wet earth.

"Good! He must have been right on schedule," Matt told her calmly as they rode up to the porch. "He had to check the fencing on the east boundary, so I told him just to leave the stuff out on the stoop and we'd put it away."

She smiled at him. "There should be plenty of time for that. Imagine . . . ten whole days of eating and sleeping and fishing and . . ."

". . . Starting to put together some lecture notes for next quarter," he said solemnly.

She glanced at him with sudden dissappoint-ment. "Matt, do you have to . . ." she broke off as she saw his lips twitch. "You're no darned good," she scolded, "I thought you were seri-ous."

They pulled in their mounts at the corral fence and dismounted.

"Let me have your reins," he said, "and I'll turn the horses in here for a while. They can be unsaddled later."

"Fine. I'll start putting the provisions away. We'd better get the perishables down to the stream."

She was kneeling on the porch, scrabbling among the packs when he came up the steps a few minutes later.

"What's the matter?" he teased. "I thought you'd have the coffee water on by now."

She searched through the end bundle, sank back on her heels, and looked up at him. "It's no use . . . it just isn't here."

"What?"

"My new sleeping bag. Don't you remember? I told you how I'd packed it so I wouldn't get cold and . . ." Her voice trailed off awkwardly. "You did tell Jake to pick it up, didn't you?" It was difficult to face his amused eyes so she addressed the toe of his riding boot.

He reached down and pulled her gently to her feet. Holding onto her arm with one hand, he leaned over and pushed open the cabin door with the other. Then, effortlessly, he swung her up into his arms and carried her over the threshold. Once into the room, he closed the door with his shoulder.

Still suspended in his arms, Di felt her breathing quicken until the heartbeats seemed loud enough to be heard across the room.

"Did you . . ." to her annoyance she had difficulty speaking and had to clear her throat before she could get the sentence out. "Did you ask Jake to pick it up?" she persisted.

He pretended to think it over carefully as he held her in his strong arms. "I guess I must have forgotten," he drawled finally.

"Forgotten?" Her voice rose in surprise. "You!" Her eyes met his in sudden suspicion and fell before their laughter.

"I'm certainly sorry about that," his tone was gently mocking. "Must have had too many things on my mind." His arm tightened around her as if suddenly impatient with the silence between them.

"I wonder," she whispered unevenly, "what we should do about it?"

Her sentence was stopped abruptly by his lips, pressed hard and possessively against hers in a long, thorough kiss that seemed to pull her down into a deep tidal pool of desire and finally left her clinging shakily to his shoulders.

Minutes, or was it eons later, he lifted his head long enough to whisper roughly against her cheek. "Don't worry, darling. Remember what I told you . . . in case of emergencies, we just make do with the materials at hand."